"Maybe you'd better stay here, Wishbone," Joe said.

Wishbone dutifully wagged his tail. "Thanks, Joe, but I know my doggie duty. It's you and me, buddy, side by side, to the bitter end."

Joe cautiously opened the gate. He stepped through, and Wishbone slipped inside, too. Joe didn't seem to notice him. All his attention was focused on the flag-stone path. At the end of it were six steps leading up to the porch and the big, dark brown mahogany front door.

Suddenly, the big bulldog came tearing around the house, bounding along in giant leaps. He gave one deep-throated  bark. Wishbone had no time to think. Acting instinctively, he threw himself forward, crouching, ready to protect Joe. . . .

The Adventures of **wishBone**™
titles in Large-Print Editions:

The Adventures of WISHBONE™

BE A WOLF!

by Brad Strickland
Inspired by *Beowulf*
by Anonymous

WISHBONE™ created by Rick Duffield

Gareth Stevens Publishing
MILWAUKEE

This book is a work of fiction. The characters, incidents, and dialogues are products of the author's imagination and are not to be construed as real. Any resemblance to actual events or persons, living or dead, is entirely coincidental.

For a free color catalog describing Gareth Stevens' list of high-quality books and multimedia programs, call 1-800-542-2595 (USA) or 1-800-461-9120 (Canada). Gareth Stevens Publishing's Fax: (414) 225-0377.

Library of Congress Cataloging-in-Publication Data

Strickland, Brad.
    Be a wolf! / by Brad Strickland.
       p. cm.
    Originally published: Allen, Texas; Big Red Chair Books, © 1997.
    (The adventures of Wishbone; #1)
       Summary: When Joe and Wishbone must confront a scary neighbor who owns a big mean dog, Wishbone imagines himself as the hero Beowulf of Geatland who helps King Hrothgar rid his kingdom of the terrible monster Grendel and his equally fearsome mother.
       ISBN 0-8368-2297-8 (lib. bdg.)
       [1. Dogs—Fiction. 2. Heroes—Fiction. 3. Adventure and adventurers—Fiction.]
    I. Beowulf. II. Title. III. Series: Adventures of Wishbone; #1.
    PZ7.S9166Bg   1999
    [Fic]—dc21   98-47162

This edition first published in 1999 by
Gareth Stevens Publishing
1555 North RiverCenter Drive, Suite 201
Milwaukee, Wisconsin 53212 USA

© 1997 Big Feats! Entertainment. First published by Big Red Chair Books™, a Division of Lyrick Publishing™, 300 E. Bethany Drive, Allen, Texas 75002.

Edited by Kevin Ryan
Copy edited by Jonathon Brodman
Cover design by Lyle Miller
Interior illustrations by Don Punchatz
Cover concept by Kathryn Yingling
Wishbone photograph by Carol Kaelson

Printed in the United States of America

1 2 3 4 5 6 7 8 9 03 02 01 00 99   DELHI TOWNSHIP

To the world's greatest second graders:
Alma, Karla, Anthony, Zap, Yesica, Jeffrey,
Tiffany, Gonzalo, Eduardo, Michelle, Shane,
Ashley, José, Liseth, Levi, Marquis, and Santos

FROM THE BIG RED CHAIR . . .

Oh . . . hi! Wishbone here. You caught me right
in the middle of some of my favorite things—books.
Let me welcome you to my brand-new book series,
THE ADVENTURES OF WISHBONE. In each of these
books I have adventures with my friends in Oakdale and
imagine myself as a character in one of the greatest stories
of all time. In *BE A WOLF!*, I imagine I'm the great warrior-
hero Beowulf, from the epic English poem *BEOWULF*—an
exciting tale about fighting monsters and dragons,
and saving kingdoms.

You're in for a real treat, so pull up
a chair and a snack and enjoy reading!

Chapter One

"Come on, Joe, watch me! It's easy!" With every muscle straining, Wishbone ran six speedy steps, then leaped up into the air, spinning completely around. The frisky white dog landed on the damp sidewalk facing Joe Talbot, his brown-haired best friend. "There! See? Easy!"

"Hey, Talbot," said Joe's tall, gangly friend Sean McMurdo with a laugh, "your dog's got the moves!"

Wishbone grinned up at this obviously intelligent young man. "Thank you. I owe it all to exercise, clean living, and eating five or six square meals a day."

"I know," Joe replied, reaching down to scratch Wishbone's ears. "But I'm interested in *basketball* moves, Sean. I have to learn that great layup of yours."

"No problem," Sean said. "We'll practice in the driveway until you can fly like an eagle."

Wishbone agreed wholeheartedly. "Wings of the eagle! Eyes of the terrier!" He went running ahead of the two boys, unable to contain his delight. Oakdale had suffered through six and a half days of miserable, misty rain—not a downpour, but just enough dampness to make going outside uncomfortable. For almost a whole week, Wishbone had been cooped up inside while Ellen, Joe's mom, worked at the library and Joe was in school.

It had been a frustrating period. Oh, Wishbone had lots of time for good books, but a dog needs to get out now and then, too. What could he do when the ground was so wet that digging in it was no fun at all? When the tall grass brushed his tummy and got his fur all cold and clammy? When Ellen became upset just because Wishbone left a few neat little pawprints on the way from the door to the food dish?

Wishbone had no choice but to stay inside a lot and yearn to breathe free. Finally the rain ended, and Wishbone was a dog happy to be outside—even if the ground still squished under his paws. It was a cool Friday afternoon, and Joe and Sean were heading over

to Sean's house to shoot some hoops. Joe wore his blue windbreaker, jeans, and sneakers. He carried his backpack over one shoulder. Sean, who was twelve, the same age as Joe but almost a head taller, was wearing a sloppy oversized red sweatshirt, jeans with stylish holes in the knees, and a beat-up pair of red sneakers that he called his lucky shoes. His own red-and-black backpack had one broken strap, and he swung it along by the other one. Sean wasn't an all-around great basketball player. Despite his spectacular layup shot, he wasn't very good at moving the ball. Joe *was* good at that, so the two figured they could practice together and both would improve their game.

"Here's my house," Sean said. He lowered his voice and added, "Oh—beware of the monster."

Wishbone's ears pricked up. "Monster? Monster?" He instantly visualized an alley cat six feet tall. The inquisitive dog looked up. "Uh . . . you *are* kidding, aren't you, Sean?"

Joe grinned at his friend in a puzzled way. "You're kidding," he said.

Wishbone sighed. No one ever listened to the dog.

Ducking his head and lowering his voice, Sean said, "Only a little. No fooling—Mrs. Grindle really scares me. She lives next door to us. I kind of got in trouble once or twice when I accidentally bounced a ball over her fence or made too much noise and she yelled at me. Not that she has to yell. One dirty look from her would stop a clock."

Wishbone sniffed. "Oh. A clock-stopper, huh?" He looked up at Joe. "Don't worry, Joe. Just stay out of her way, and she'll stay out of yours."

Sean lived in a one-story brick house, the second one on the left on Norman Street. It was easy to see where Mrs. Grindle lived. A black mailbox had her name on it—"Thelma Grindle." Her place was a three-story Victorian frame house, its paint faded to a dingy yellow-white. A porch ran across the front. On the left, an octagonal tower rose one story higher than the rest of the house. The roof was steep, and around the edges were gingerbread decorations: fancy wooden circles, triangles, ovals, and other shapes. The yard was overgrown with knee-high grass and brushy, unpruned rosebushes. A peeling white picket fence encircled the yard. The place certainly looked ominous enough, maybe one step away from being a haunted house.

Wishbone's nose twitched. Someone besides Mrs. Grindle lived in there—a very big dog. Everything was quiet, but as Wishbone stared at the old house, he saw something that made the fur on his neck bristle. A curtain in a downstairs window whisked aside, and the pale blur of a face glared out.

Wishbone barked an alarm. Joe looked down. "What's wrong, boy?"

"Look up there." Wishbone pointed with his nose. He blinked. The curtain was back in place. "Too late. You missed it."

Joe shook his head. "Glad to be outside, aren't you?"

Wishbone gave the window another long, suspicious look. "Ask me again later."

Sean had tossed his backpack down and picked up a basketball that lay beneath the hoop. He bounced it a few times and informed Joe, "My mom won't be home until later, and Dad's on a sales trip until next week. Want to shoot some baskets now?"

"No time like the present," Joe replied with a grin.

The driveway of Sean's house ran right alongside Mrs. Grindle's picket fence. At the far end, Sean and his dad had set up a basketball hoop on a pole beside the garage. It was perfect—regulation height—and the driveway was so wide that there was almost a half-court to practice on.

"Let me see that layup again," Joe told Sean.

Grinning, Sean dribbled the ball, approached the basket in a graceful curving run, then took to the air like a bird. He turned as he rose, dunked the ball expertly, and came back to earth.

Wishbone scratched his ear with his left hind foot. "Not bad, not bad at all. But throw me my red plastic flying saucer and I can match it!" He glanced at the house next door, then growled a little when he noticed the same curtain dropping back into place. The spy was at it again!

Sean retrieved the ball and tossed it back to Joe. "Nothing to it, man," Sean said. "In no time we'll have you sinking 'em as if you had wings."

Joe shook his head, his expression rueful. "I don't know. But I'm sure going to give it my best try!" He shrugged out of his brand-new backpack and looked around. On the pavement, Sean's battered backpack already looked damp. "I don't want to put this on the ground. I'm going to hang it on the fence, okay?"

Wishbone stared at him. "Hang it on the *fence?* When some kind of monster keeps spying on us? It could be in danger! I know—let's bury it! I'll help you dig!"

Sean looked past the fence at the old three-story Victorian house. "Uh . . . sure," he muttered. "I guess that will be okay." He took a deep breath as he watched Joe loop one of the backpack's straps over a couple of pickets. The backpack hung against the fence, high and dry.

Turning, Joe raised his eyebrows at his friend's strange expression. "What's wrong, Sean?"

Sean shook his head. "Nothing, nothing. All right, Talbot, let's see what you've got. Take a good start and then do your layup."

Wishbone found a fairly dry spot under the overhang of the garage and sat on the pavement. "That's right, Joe. Coach Wishbone is here, ready to give you his advice. All right now, guys, I want to see some hustle!"

For more than half an hour, Sean and Joe practiced. In all the excitement, Wishbone forgot to keep a lookout on the house next door. He trotted eagerly alongside the driveway, barking encouragement. Sometimes he sat alertly on his dry spot, following the quick action with rapid jerks of his head. At first Joe just couldn't get that snappy little twist that always brought Sean sailing right up to the basket. He was either a little too quick on the turn so that he was already too far around at the top of his jump, or a little too slow so he wasn't quite in position for the shot.

But at last everything went just right. Joe's layup wasn't a dunk, because he was shorter than Sean, but it went right in the basket, not even touching the rim.

Wishbone had been sitting. He leaped to his feet and almost danced in his excitement. "Yes! I knew you could do it, Joe! Good boy! Good boy!"

"Hey," Sean said, "you got it, Talbot." He gave Joe a high five. "Now do it again." Sean turned away laughing—and froze. "Oh, man!"

"What's wrong?" Joe asked.

Wishbone followed the line of Sean's gaze. He was staring at the house—and someone was staring back. The curtain was pulled aside. A woman frowned down at them. Her dark eyebrows were drawn together in a scowl, and her mouth was set in a grim line. She quickly dropped the curtain and vanished behind it.

"Was that her?" Joe croaked, swallowing hard. "She looks angry."

"That's Mrs. Grindle," Sean told his friend. "We were probably making too much noise or something. Now she'll call my mom and I'll get bawled out." He sighed. "Maybe we'd better quit now."

Wishbone's head snapped around. "What? Quit just because someone mean and nasty is staring at you? Come on, guys—where's your courage?"

13

"Okay," Joe agreed. "I don't want to get you in trouble."

Tossing the ball over to the corner of the garage, Sean shook his head. "Man, when we moved in here I was eight years old. My dad saw Mrs. Grindle as we were unloading the moving van, and he told her that he hoped we would be good neighbors. She snapped back, 'Just make sure you stay on your side of the fence!' I don't think my folks have talked to her since—except when she calls up to complain about something I do that bothers her."

"Want to go for a soda or something?" Joe asked.

Sean checked his watch. "Sure. As long as we get back by five. Mom should be home about then. At least I'll keep out of the monster's hair for that long."

Wishbone's ears perked up. "A soda? May I recommend Pepper Pete's Pizza parlor? I admire its service, its food, and its affection for handsome dogs!"

Joe said, "Let's take a walk down to Pepper Pete's."

Wishbone's tail wagged happily. "That's my boy!"

They walked down Norman Street, and at the corner, Wishbone barked a joyful greeting. He saw two friends strolling the same way they were headed—Sam and David! Wishbone ran up to greet them.

"Hi, Wishbone!" Samantha Kepler—"Sam" for short—leaned over to scratch Wishbone's head.

"Hi, Sam! Mmm, great! Now the left ear, please. You're the best ear scratcher in Oakdale!"

"Wishbone, buddy," David Barnes said. He chuckled. "You've made him happy, Sam."

Wishbone liked Sam a lot. She shared his love for adventure and his curiosity about everything. As for David, he was practically a genius at making things. He showed you what someone with thumbs could really do when he put his mind to it! "Hi, David! Glad you're here. I've got great news, guys—a terrific accomplishment! *I* have taught Joe how to do a fantastic layup shot!"

Joe said, "Hi, guys. We're on our way to the pizza parlor. Sean was just teaching me how to do his patented layup."

Wishbone looked over his shoulder. "Well, yes, he helped a little. But I was coaching!"

"Cool," David replied.

"So what are you two doing?" Sean asked, coming up behind Joe.

Sam shrugged. "Not much. Just enjoying being outside after a week of rain."

Joe nodded his understanding. "Want to come along with us?"

Wishbone darted ahead. "Come on, gang—let's race!"

Sam laughed. "Sure, let's go. But I'm not running."

Wishbone trotted beside them, breathing deep sniffs of cool, damp air. The pizza parlor smelled even better. Mmm—sausage, hamburger, pepperoni, anchovies. As usual, Wishbone managed to look hungry enough to get several tasty tidbits. Then he lay down beside Joe's chair and began to plan what he would do the next day. Saturdays were always fun! "Let me see:

Wake up, stretch, check out the backyard to see what's going on, go back inside, have some breakfast, play with Joe, nap, get up, have a snack, dig in Wanda's yard, come home, have a snack, nap, get up, have lunch. . . ." It would be a great day, he thought.

Then the kids came out of the pizza parlor and they all went back to Sean's house. Sean's mom had just pulled her station wagon into the driveway. Sean, Sam, David, and Joe helped her unload a week's worth of groceries. When they had finished, Joe said goodbye, and the group split up.

Wishbone was still thinking about Saturday as he and Joe went into their house. Ellen, Joe's mom, was already cooking dinner, but she had time to toss Wishbone a couple of Doggie Ginger Snaps, which he crunched happily. "Much homework this weekend, Joe?" she asked.

Joe, who had been setting the table, froze, then slapped his palm against his forehead. "Oh, no!"

Wishbone looked up from his doggie treat. "Whassa matta?" He swallowed with a gulp. "Excuse me. What's the matter?"

"I left my backpack over at Sean's house," Joe said. "I'd better call him and ask him to take it inside." He went to the phone and spoke to Sean for about five minutes. After he finished his phone call, Joe had a miserable expression. "I think I'm in trouble, Mom," he said, his voice hesitant.

Wishbone sat at Joe's feet and looked up. "Trouble? Tell us about it."

Ellen raised her eyebrows. "What is it?"

Joe looked down. "I sort of hung my backpack on the fence that belongs to Sean's next-door neighbor. Sean said that when he went out to look for it just now, it was gone."

"Oh, Joe," Ellen said. "Well, you'll just have to go look for it."

"That's the problem," Joe told her. "Sean's neighbor must have picked it up."

"Then you can just go and ask about it," Ellen said.

"That's just it—I can't," Joe answered, sounding truly worried. "Sean says she's a real monster."

"I'm sure it's not that bad. Now dinner's almost ready," Ellen said. "Let's talk about this later. Go wash your hands."

Wishbone followed Joe through the house. Joe looked down at his canine friend and sighed. "Now what am I going to do?"

Wishbone considered the question. *Hmm,* he thought. *Something about all this seems strangely familiar. A real monster takes something from Joe, and he's nervous about getting it back. And her name is Mrs. Grindle. Now, where have I heard something like that before?*

Joe went into the bathroom to wash his hands, and Wishbone trotted over to a bookcase. He pawed at some books on the lowest shelf until a tall, slim, green volume slipped out and fell open. It was just the one he was looking for.

Oh, yes, this is it! The story of *Beowulf*! It's a

17

tale of high adventure, fights with monsters, and great courage. It's one of the oldest stories in the English language. Researchers believe that it was made up more than a thousand years ago, about 750 A.D. It was eventually written down much later, sometime around the year 950 A.D. The poem is composed in a very hard-to-read version of the English language called Old English, and it's a hero-ic tale. It shows you that sometimes you have to face terrible odds with great courage. Sometimes it's just not enough to be a tame dog. You have to listen to the call of the wild! You have to be like your remote ancestors! Sometimes you have to be a wolf!

Wishbone licked his nose and turned pages until he found a picture he remembered. He stared at the colorful illustration. It was a Viking dragon ship, long and sleek, with one square sail. Rows of round shields hung on the sides. In the ship were fur-clad Norse war-riors, wearing conical helmets with horns attached to them, and those men pulled on long oars. In the front of the ship, behind the carved prow that looked like a dragon's head, stood a tall, strong young warrior, Beowulf.

Even though *Beowulf* is an Old English poem, it isn't about English people and places. The hero is a member of a Scandinavian tribe called the Geats. Their homeland was in the country that we call Sweden today. The Geats, whose king at the time was named Hygelac, were related to many other tribes, including the Danes. That was why Beowulf, a young cousin of King Hygelac, decided to go to help Hrothgar, the king of the Danes, when news of the monster Grendel reached Geat-Land.

As Wishbone stared at the picture, he began to imagine that he *was* Beowulf, bold and brave, crossing the sea to help a king who needed a hero. The curious dog imagined the foggy moisture of the sea cool in his fur. The salty, fishy smell of the ocean seemed sharp in his nose. The sound of the dipping oars created a steady rhythm in his ears, as the dragon ship glided along. Yes, ahead somewhere in the land of Denmark, King Hrothgar had an awful problem—a problem involving an uncivilized, terrible, man-eating monster named . . . Grendel.

Sometimes, Wishbone thought again, *you have to be a wolf!*

Chapter Two

After a long two days and nights of sailing, the dragon ship glided through a still world. The sea was gray and glassy, and the fog was just as gray. The wind had been favorable, but during the early morning it had died away, leaving the ship motionless in the fog. There was only one thing to do. The crew had to row the rest of the way to their landing site.

The Geat warriors, fourteen of them, pulled at the long oars, while Beowulf stood in the bow of the ship, his keen eyes and nose searching ahead. He rested his front paws on the rail, trying to stare through the fog, straining to catch sight of the hills of Denmark, their destination. To encourage his men, he wagged his tail, giving them the best rowing rhythm.

Everything was gray—the sea and sky had dissolved into one vague blur. Overhead, invisible, gulls soared and screamed their shrill cries. Beowulf paid them no attention. His ears twitched forward, listening for another sound, for the clue that would tell him land was near. At last it came to him, a regular, low roaring, like the sound he imagined one of the legendary frost-giants would make if he were deep asleep and breathing slowly.

"We're getting close," he barked back over his shoulder. "I can hear surf not far off, and I smell trees and green grass. Courage, my men! Row strongly! The end of our voyage is near!"

Behind him the men rowed obediently, their muscular arms straining to drive the ship ahead. Beowulf leaned forward, every sense alert, his fur almost standing on end. The fog began to grow thinner, glowing with a pearly light. Above the ship, a patch of blue sky revealed itself, and a white gull with

black-tipped wings flashed overhead and then was gone. Then Beowulf could finally see the ocean, gray-green and gently rolling. Moments later the dragon-headed ship broke through the stubborn fog bank, and ahead lay a rugged coast, dark against the pale blue sky of morning.

"Denmark!" Beowulf called with excitement. "Well done, my men! I'm proud of you. Not one of you asked, 'Are we there yet?' "

The crew let loose with a loud cheer. Then they rowed with even more enthusiasm. Beowulf sniffed. Above the salty smell of ocean, he caught the scent of horses and of men. Straining his eyes, he saw one distant, dark figure atop the hills. It was a man sitting on a horse, gripping a spear in his right hand.

"I see the shore-guard of Hrothgar!" Beowulf announced to his men. "Hrothgar must be a good king. He keeps careful watch."

"But what will he think of us?" asked Wingard, one of Beowulf's best warriors. "Surely he will see that we are a ship of fighting men. He'll think Denmark is being invaded!"

Without looking around, Beowulf shook his head. "No. Though we are great fighters, there are only fifteen of us. Hrothgar's guard would realize that a raiding party would be a greater force."

"There is none greater than you among the Geats, my lord," the loyal Wingard replied respectfully.

"You are a very perceptive man," Beowulf said.

"But of course, the Danes may not agree with you—
and they don't even know who we are yet. Row, my
friends, row for the shore!"

Half an hour passed. The long ship drew nearer
and nearer to the beach, until Beowulf could clearly
see the sandy, pebbly shore. The man on horseback,
now joined by seven others, was making his way
down a winding track to meet them. Beowulf
stretched his front legs and then his rear legs, working out the stiffness of cramped days and nights
aboard ship. It would be good, he thought, to get out
of the ship at last. He wanted to feel earth beneath
his paws and to work the kinks out of all his muscles.
Even his tail felt tense after two days at sea! He could
tell that the guardsmen would reach the beach at
about the same time as the ship. Good! Beowulf
approved of a king who kept alert guards. A wise man
chooses the best watchdogs! Hrothgar was no fool,
and that was good to know. All that remained was to
watch the waves, waiting for the precise moment
when the rowers could make the ship glide safely up
onto the beach.

"Now!" shouted the young warrior, judging the
time exactly. The men strained at their oars, and the
ship seemed to leap forward with a life of its own, like
a young dog who had just spotted a prowling alley cat.
Beneath Beowulf's paws the hull ground up into the
sand with a long noise like *tt-ss-chuuchhh!* Immediately
Wingard and six other men leaped ashore and hauled
the ship up onto the beach.

Beowulf jumped down to the sand. He looked up. Far along the beach, seven of the riders waited in a loose formation. The eighth man rode forward alone, holding his spear over his head and shaking it to show that he wanted to talk, not fight. The rider wore a helmet and chain mail—a knee-length coat of armor made of steel links woven together. His ruddy face showed determination and courage.

He reined in his great white horse and stared at the graceful ship and the warriors. "I am in command of the coast-guard," he said. "I serve Hrothgar, king of the Danes. Strangers, no ship of warriors may make a landfall here without my lord's permission. I don't know you or your ship—you are not Danes, nor kin of the king's. But one of you"—he nodded to Beowulf—"looks to be as strong a warrior as any I have ever seen. Tell me who you are, and what your business is."

Beowulf stepped forward, his ears alert, his chin and tail held high. "You keep a sharp watch," he replied. "I am the leader of these men. Your king knew my father well. My father's name was Ectheow, a prince among the Geats. He has now gone to his rest, and I, his son, have brought these warriors to Denmark to help your leader." Beowulf paused. If the guard was well trained, he would not ask Beowulf's name—that was for Hrothgar to know, not his soldiers. The guard remained silent, truly a warrior who knew the proper ways of doing things. Feeling even more respect for this guardsman, Beowulf continued: "Fate has brought us here to fight beside the Danes. We have heard that your king, Hrothgar, son of Halfdane, is having trouble with a monster, something called Grendel."

The guard drew himself up. "What are the troubles of the Danes to the Geats?" he demanded.

The lordly Beowulf replied, "Work with me here, okay? Look, we don't know who or what Grendel is, but we've come to help Hrothgar dispose of him. Take us to your king, and I'll offer him our services as monster busters. Is that fair?"

With a surprised look on his face, the Dane responded, "Your men have come to help us fight the monster?"

Beowulf nodded. "Let's just say we've come to fight the monster for you—if Hrothgar will accept our offer."

"Why would you risk your life?" the guard asked.

"For fame! For glory!" Beowulf said proudly.

"For reward?" the guard asked. "I'm sure Hrothgar would be generous to anyone who could rid him of Grendel."

Beowulf shrugged. "Okay, for reward, too, then. If we defeat Grendel, and Hrothgar has any valuables lying around—gold, pearls, porterhouse steaks, stuff like that—sure, he can give them to us. But let's leave that up to him. Now, will you take us to the king so we can ask him if he wants our help?"

For a moment the horseman thought. Then he came to a decision and nodded. "A good soldier needs to know the difference between words and actions," he said. "Something tells me that you're the sort of leader who will do what he says. Very well! Come with me, and I will take you and all your men to Heorot, the great hall that Hrothgar has built. He keeps his court there, for it is safe enough in the daytime. The monster comes only at night."

Beowulf blinked. "Uh . . . excuse me? Helllooo? The monster comes right into the throne room? You *do* need our help! All right, let me make sure the ship is okay, and we'll be right with you."

But the guard waved to his men, who came galloping forward. "There is no need, leader of the Geats. My men will make sure your dragon-ship is safely moored, and they will guard it, keeping it safe until you return."

"Well, that's mighty neighborly of you," Beowulf said. "Lead on!"

Beowulf and his men followed the horseman up a winding path to the hilltops, then along a narrow dirt track.

While they're making their way to the king, let me explain a few things. The poem *Beowulf* isn't anything like modern poetry. It's not rhymed, for one thing. Instead, the poem uses a trick of language called "alliteration." That means that two or more words in each line have to start with the same sound. It goes like this:

<u>H</u>earing <u>h</u>ow the <u>h</u>ateful ogre <u>h</u>armed <u>H</u>rothgar's <u>h</u>all,

Beowulf, <u>b</u>right helmet gleaming, <u>b</u>egan his <u>b</u>old journey,

With <u>c</u>ourage <u>k</u>een, the <u>k</u>ingly <u>c</u>ur did sail—

"Cur?" Wait a minute, I'm not a cur! Hmm— this alliteration stuff is harder than it looks. Oh, well, let's see how Beowulf and his men are doing.

The green fields of Denmark spread out on both sides of the marching Geats. Sheep grazed contentedly, and here and there, stone shepherds' huts dotted the landscape. The track eventually became a paved road. At last, hours after the men had begun their long journey, they saw in the distance a town, consisting of a cluster of wooden buildings.

The horseman drew in his steed and pointed ahead with his spear. "There is my lord's dwelling," he said. "Hrothgar will be in the great mead-hall called Heorot. You will know it by the many deer antlers decorating its walls. Go straight there and ask for the king. As for me, I must return to my duties before sunset, so I will bid you farewell."

"Uh-huh. Thank you, my good man," Beowulf replied. When the guard had ridden off, he said, "Well, you heard our friend. Come on! We have only about five miles or so to go."

"I wish we had horses," Wingard complained.

"If wishes were horses, Geats would ride," Beowulf replied. "But they aren't, so shake a few legs."

Now that they were closer to a town, houses began to appear near the road. People working in gardens or drawing water from wells paused to gaze at the fifteen armored men marching forward.

"What are they staring at?" Beowulf asked.

"Your helmet, my lord," replied the loyal Wingard.

"Oh. Well, it *is* handsome," Beowulf said. It was true. His helmet was fashioned of bright bronze, with likenesses of wild boars—the symbol of his family—attached to it above the visor.

After another hour of quick marching, the troop at last came into the town. One-story wooden buildings clustered around a central square, and on a hilltop just beyond the square stood Heorot, the great hall built by King Hrothgar. It was a wonderful building indeed—tall, steep-roofed, and solid, with row upon row of stags' antlers running around the wall beneath the eaves. The wooden beams had been carved to resemble dragons, warriors, and other figures. Gold and silver inlays made the woodwork gleam in the sunlight. Right at that moment, however, tired as he was, Beowulf saw something even more attractive—a place to sit.

Benches had been placed along the outside walls. They looked like a fine, sunny place to rest. Near the massive front door, not far from the benches, stood a guard in shining armor. Beowulf led his weary band forward.

"Halt!" the guard ordered. "Warriors, I am Wulfgar, advisor to King Hrothgar. Why are you coming to his hall dressed for battle?"

Beowulf, hot and weary after the long march, resisted the impulse to bark at the guard. After all, Wulfgar was just doing his duty. "Noble Wulfgar," Beowulf said, "we are Geats, and in our far-off land we heard about Grendel, yatta-yatta-yatta, and the bottom line is that we want to ask King Hrothgar if we can help."

"Indeed, you speak like a hero, leader of the Geats," replied Wulfgar. "Sit here, rest, and I will ask the king if he will see you." He went inside the hall.

Beowulf turned to his men. "Okay, fellows, you heard him. Take five." From inside his mail shirt he pulled a savory soup bone. "Chew 'em if you got 'em."

His men sank gratefully onto the benches with sighs of relief. Townspeople were collecting now, staring at the strangers and whispering. Beowulf nodded to them as he chewed his snack. He looked around. The community was a prosperous place, he could tell, but it had an air of sadness about it, too, as if the folk had suffered for a long time. Beowulf wondered exactly what was causing their misery. All the Geats had heard was the name "Grendel," and they had been told that it was a terrible creature of some kind. Well, Fate would tell Beowulf, sooner or later.

Beowulf believed strongly in Fate. *Wyrd* was the name that his people gave to this force. Fate determined if a warrior would live or die in a battle. Until a fighter's Fate decreed it was his time to die, he would not die, but when his time had come, nothing could save him. All a warrior could do was to live honorably and fight with bravery, trusting to *wyrd* and doing his best.

"King Hrothgar will see you," a voice announced.

Beowulf got to his feet and thrust the half-chewed bone into his mail shirt. Maybe he could bury it later. "Come on, Geats," he called to his men. "We're playing the palace!"

Inside, Heorot was just as magnificent as it was outside. The floor was on two levels, and in the center of the building was a great open space, where feasts could be prepared in celebration of a successful battle. Beowulf didn't notice that. Instead, his eyes were fixed on a strongly built man, with a long gray beard and gray hair, who was seated on a chair that was lavishly inlaid with gold and ivory. Guards and other attendants stood close to him. This, Beowulf realized, must be the king.

Beowulf and his men approached, and Beowulf bowed, stretching his front paws far out and courteously lowering his head until his chin rested on his front legs.

The king nodded. "Rise, prince of the Geats. I am Hrothgar, king of the Danes. My advisor, Wulfgar, tells me you have come to help us in our troubles."

"We have, my lord," Beowulf replied. "I am Beowulf, a subject of King Hygelac of the Geats, and I am the son of Ectheow. When my father was in his youth, you helped him."

A smile crossed the old king's face. "I did indeed. I remember it well. He had killed a man in a duel, and the man's relatives had sworn vengeance. I paid Ectheow's fine for him and gave him shelter. He was a good friend. His son is welcome here."

"I have come to kill Grendel for you," Beowulf announced boldly.

The old king sighed. "I think no warrior can do that. When I built Heorot, little did I know that in the swamps outside town there lurked a monster, Grendel. People say he is descended from Cain, the first murderer. He is an ogre and a cannibal. Much bigger and stronger than any man, he forces his way into this hall if anyone sleeps in it by night. He attacks my soldiers and devours them. My men do not dare stay here after sunset. This monster, Grendel, has disgraced me and my army." With misery in his voice, the old king added, "A king who cannot protect his warriors, even in the mead-hall he built for them, knows how bitter life can be. I feel a very deep sense of shame, young Beowulf."

"Say no more," said Beowulf, looking as fierce as a wolfhound. "My Geats and I will take care of this ogre for you. We won't ask for your help. Let us face him alone, and we will succeed. If Fate is against us and we fail, why, you won't have to worry about giving us a funeral, because Grendel will eat us! Right, Wingard?"

Wingard gave a weak smile and swallowed hard. "Uh . . . yes, my lord."

"That's the spirit! Danes, Geats, listen to my boast: I, Beowulf, will fight this Grendel in single combat. Either he or I will die tonight. May Fate favor me!"

"That is quite a boast," said an unpleasant, sneering voice, "especially from someone who failed once before."

Beowulf growled in anger. "Who said that?"

A wiry man stepped forward. He was short and stringy and disagreeable-looking. "I, Unferth, one of my lord Hrothgar's best warriors," he replied proudly. "Beowulf, I have heard that in your youth you boasted you were the best swimmer in the world, and you and your friend Breca had a swimming contest. But he won, and your boast was empty."

Beowulf felt like snarling at this mangy cur of a man. "You didn't hear the whole story," he said coldly. "It's true, Breca and I did have a great swimming race. Both of us wore armor, and each of us carried a sword, and both of us plunged into the icy sea at the same moment. Breca struck out with a powerful crawl stroke, while I parted the seas with my skilled dog paddle. For seven long days we swam, and it's true that Breca arrived on shore a few moments before I did—but he didn't have to fight off any sea monsters!"

"Sea monsters?" Hrothgar echoed in amazement.

"Thou betteth thy life, sire," Beowulf responded. "They swam up from the deepest of depths. Sharks, octopuses, giant squids, sea serpents, anchovies! They charged at me! They tried to drag me down!"

The king gasped. "What happened?"

Beowulf's eyes grew sharp with the memory. "Monsters to the right of me! Monsters to the left of me! Seagulls above me—well, I really didn't mind the gulls so much. As for the monsters, I drew my sword and struck at them, slashing left and then right. I cut one to pieces, then another, and another. Finally, when I had killed the last, I put on a burst of speed, but Breca came out barely ahead of me. Still, even Breca admitted that I would have won the great sea race if the monsters had not attacked." With a smile, he asked, "Have you ever done anything like that, Unferth?"

Before Unferth could speak, the king rose. "My people!" he called out. "Make Beowulf welcome! Tonight this slayer of monsters meets the greatest villain of all—Grendel! I pray that his strength may be great enough to save him, and to save us!"

Beowulf inhaled deeply, noticing smells of cooking, the faint scent of ancient blood—and the odor of fear. He could not help but shiver just a little. Even a hero could experience moments when he felt a twinge of fear. Silently, he thought, *I pray so, too, King Hrothgar. I pray so, too!*

Wishbone's Warriors' Word-Hoard

Hail, friends! Wishbone here! Since Beowulf *takes place at a time far back in history, a lot about the story seems strange. Do you wonder what Old English was like? Well, here are a few lines of* Beowulf, *as they were originally composed in Old English:*

Hroxgar mazelode helm sc&ldinga
ic hine cuxe cniht wesende waes his
ealdfaeder Ecgzeow haten. . . .

Wow! Hard to read, isn't it? Can you find the name of King Hrothgar and of Ectheow, Beowulf's father? Some of the words look very odd. Fear not, however, good friends, for Wishbone will open his word-hoard to you. That's a fancy Old English way of saying "Here are strange words and their definitions!"

chain mail: A flexible armor made of many small steel chain links that were woven together. A chain-mail

	shirt was very heavy, and it had to be worn over a thick protective piece of cloth or a leather jacket.
fen:	A deep, open pool of water in low, swampy country.
mead:	A drink made from fermented honey. Generous kings like Hrothgar built mead-halls in which their men could relax between battles. In fact, Heorot is one of these mead-halls.
scop:	A poet who sings songs about great heroes—like Beowulf.
thane:	A loyal nobleman who serves his king.
wyrd:	Fate. It determines whether a warrior lives or dies in battle. It is also the ancestor of our modern-day word "weird."

Now, on with the story. As the sun sank low in the sky, King Hrothgar commanded his people to honor Beowulf and his men with a great feast. Yum! Excuse me while I see if there's anything nice and munchy on the table—or even under it. I'm not picky!

Chapter Three

As Beowulf's men feasted, he sat silently, think-ing deep thoughts, his tail wagging slowly. The prospect of fighting a fearsome battle lay before him, and took away his appetite. He only pawed at his food, having just three helpings of everything instead of his usual five or six. Hrothgar's scop, the court poet, sang songs of battle and glory. Hrothgar and his queen, Wealtheow, were generous and kind to the Geats. Of the whole court, only Unferth seemed distrustful of the visitors. Everyone else wished Beowulf and his men well.

The afternoon drew to a close. As the sun sank in the west, Beowulf noticed Hrothgar's people glancing fearfully to the south—the land of the fens, a boggy countryside filled with many deep, mysterious pools of stagnant water. That was Grendel's home, and everyone knew that as soon as it was dark, the monster would come out on a raid. Even Beowulf's men began to seem nervous. Deciding that he had to put some bravery in them, Beowulf stood up in his chair, bracing his paws on the table in front of him. "I have something to say!" he announced.

Everyone grew silent. All eyes turned to the noble warrior.

Beowulf gave them all a grim smile. "Listen! In the past, Grendel has caused you much harm. Your warriors have told us how he has killed dozens of men, ripping them to shreds with his strong claws. We have heard how he eats the bodies. Well, the terror of Grendel ends tonight! You have the Geats to fight for you now."

Beowulf looked around, thinking to himself, *Uh-huh! That's got their attention. But I see a few doubts nagging away at them all, like a flea in a spot you just can't reach.* He decided it was time for a boast. When facing long odds, warriors always boasted of the great deeds they would do. That psyched them up. A warrior who bragged and then did not follow up and accomplish what he had promised was someone to make mock of and to scorn. No self-respecting warrior would go back on a boast, or he'd end up with his tail between his legs.

"Danes!" Beowulf called in his loudest voice. "I will show this evil Grendel that he isn't as strong as he thinks. We Geats will sleep in Heorot tonight, waiting for Grendel to come. When he does, I will fight with him mano a mano! Monster-against-hero combat, and may the better warrior win! See here, I will take my great sword from my belt. Grendel uses no weapons except his claws and his grip. So with teeth and grip I will fight him! Let Fate decide tonight who deserves to live and who deserves to die!"

"Brave words, Beowulf!" cried King Hrothgar, lifting a cup of mead in a toast. His queen, Wealtheow, rose from her place and with her own hands brought a cup of the golden liquid to Beowulf. That was a great honor.

"I thank you, my lord," Beowulf said humbly, returning Hrothgar's toast. "If I die in trying to perform my boast, I ask only this—let our people know that Beowulf and his band of Geats perished in battle, as warriors should."

Shadows were growing long, and the sun was almost on the rim of the world. The crowd, mumbling now, began to leave the great hall. Many of Hrothgar's warriors paused to wish the Geats good luck. "They give us fair words," Wingard said to Beowulf.

"But I notice they don't ask to stay with us," Beowulf replied with a grin.

Hrothgar remained for a long time as the evening came on. He had torches lighted, and when at last he took his leave, he offered Beowulf his hand. Beowulf put his paw in the king's grasp in a pledge of loyalty. "Beowulf," Hrothgar said, "you are indeed a worthy thane. I, Hrothgar, king of the Danes, promise you this: If you win the battle tonight and kill Grendel, I will reward you richly. You shall have all the treasure you can carry, and we Danes will honor your name for as long as memory can hold it."

"Thank you, my lord," Beowulf said. "We can ask no more."

Hrothgar turned and strode from the hall.

"There he goes," Wingard said. "Well, Beowulf, what's the plan?"

Beowulf sniffed the air. He could smell the lingering aromas of the feast, woodsmoke, and . . . something else? Something foul and sour? He couldn't be sure. "Our plan is what I boasted, my friend," he answered at last. "Let us spread out our bedrolls on the floor. We will put out all the torches, leaving the hall in darkness. They say this Grendel can sense when warriors are in the hall, and when he knows they're here, nothing can keep him from breaking in and attacking them. We'll make it easy for him—leave the door unbarred. I want every man to have his sword at hand. I will sleep unarmed, as I promised."

So the Geats settled down uneasily for the night. Beowulf took the last torch between his teeth and plunged it into a pail of water. Darkness flooded into Heorot. Only the glowing red embers of the cooking fire could be seen, and they were not bright enough to pierce the shadows. Outside an owl called mournfully, over and over. The Geats lay on the floor, waiting. For a while, they carried on low, hushed conversations, but they had just completed a long journey, and they were tired. One by one they fell asleep, until only Beowulf lay awake, his keen hearing and his sharp sense of smell straining to catch some sign of the enemy.

The night passed slowly. The Geats were snoring when Beowulf suddenly sat bolt upright, his ears twitching forward. Someone was moving outside the hall . . . someone or some *thing*.

Peering through the gloomy darkness, Beowulf felt the fur on his neck bristle. The door opened slowly, silently. There, framed in moonlight, stood a most monstrous creature. Taller by far than any mortal man, it had a huge, misshapen head, brawny arms ending in great claw-hooked hands, and two baleful red eyes that blazed even in the black of night. Washing in with the monster was a stench, sickening, a smell of dead fish and rotten mud. When it took a single step into the hall, its enormous flat foot squelched.

Beowulf began to shiver. *Steady,* he told himself silently, willing his four legs to stand their ground. *Sure, you're afraid. But courage isn't* not *being afraid. It's being afraid and doing what you have to do despite everything! Steady . . .*

The gigantic ogre crept inside. Its silence was uncanny. Only a hero with hearing as sharp as Beowulf's could have detected Grendel at all.

Beowulf felt his stomach lurch when the fiend suddenly snatched one of the sleeping warriors from the floor. With a twist of its claws, the monster wrung the unlucky man's neck, then devoured the entire body in six quick bites. The silence was the worst of all. Not one of the other Geats even stirred during the dreadful deed.

Beowulf was the next in line. Dimly he saw the

creature reach out a groping claw. The warrior was ready. Beowulf suddenly seized the monster's hand in his teeth and held it in an iron grip.

He felt the surprised Grendel try to jerk away. No use! Beowulf was famous for the steel-like strength of his grasp. Bracing his paws, he held on, just as silent as Grendel. The bizarre battle raged in the gloom of Heorot, the monster twisting and yanking, thrashing, trying to rid itself of the hero's hold. Beowulf held on, his superhuman grip firm as a glacier, his teeth set, the breath coming hard in his lungs.

Something gave. Beowulf felt something tear, and for the first time Grendel cried out, a hoarse bellow of rage and fear and pain. Twisting sharply, snapping his head to one side while his paws fought for balance, Beowulf tried to throw the mighty monster to the floor. Instead, he ripped the creature's arm from its socket!

Screaming, the injured monster lunged away. In his desperate attempt to escape, Grendel tore his arm completely off at the shoulder! Beowulf's men sprang up all around him. Shrieking in pain and fear, Grendel banged against the door frame, then lurched howling into the night.

Someone brought a torch. In its red, flickering light, Beowulf saw the scaly claw, the filthy, muscular arm of the giant Grendel. He dropped it and it fell lifeless to the floor. The monster's blood splashed all over the wood planks.

Wingard slapped Beowulf on the back. "You did

it!" he cried. "You gave that massive monster his death wound!"

Beowulf looked up. People were flooding into Heorot, Hrothgar at their head. The king stopped short when he saw the ghastly trophy. "Grendel came—he came, and you defeated him!" he cried out. "You've killed the beast!"

"Well," Beowulf said, "let's say I disarmed him!"

The cheer from the Danes was deafening. Finally, no one—not even the sour-faced Unferth—could doubt that Beowulf was a true hero.

Yes, Beowulf showed courage when he faced the unknown. My friend Joe had to search for the same kind of bravery, too. He soon learned he had his own "Grindle" to face. . . .

Chapter Four

Ellen hung up the phone. "Unfortunately," she said with a sigh, "Mrs. Grindle has an unlisted telephone number. I guess you'll just have to go over to her house tomorrow and ask her to return your backpack."

Joe made a face. "Do I have to, Mom?"

Wishbone, sitting beside Joe on the sofa, put his paw on his friend's knee. "Come on, Joe. Courage! I'll go with you."

Ellen said gently, "Joe, you have to have your backpack, don't you?"

He nodded miserably. "Yes. I've got all my books in there, and my notes for the big math test next week. I borrowed a basketball video from the P.E. teacher, and that's in there, too. I guess I'll have to go ask Mrs. Grindle for my backpack. I can't go in to school and tell everybody that I managed to lose every book I had."

"I think I know a bit about Mrs. Grindle," Ellen

46

said. "I don't believe that she's as bad as you expect her to be."

"Sean says she's awful."

"She keeps to herself, but there's no law against that. Go call Sean and see if he can tell whether she's home."

"Okay." Joe dragged himself out of the room.

Wishbone cocked his head to one side. "Okay, Ellen, come clean. What's up with this Mrs. Grindle character?"

"Want your dinner, Wishbone?" Ellen asked, getting a can of dog food from the pantry.

"I want to get to the bottom of the Grindle mystery!" Wishbone thought a moment. "Maybe right after my dinner." He ran to his bowl and waited politely until Ellen had finished spooning the food out before he began to eat.

Joe came back into the kitchen. "No luck," he said. "Sean says all the lights are out over at her house. She's probably asleep already. She's kind of old."

"You'll have to go over tomorrow, then," Ellen said. "Really, I think you're making too much of this situation. What gave you the idea that Mrs. Grindle is going to bite your head off, anyway?"

Joe shrugged. "I don't know. It's just the way Sean talks about her. He's lived next door to her for four years, ever since his family moved to Oakdale. Sometimes she stares at him without saying a word, and sometimes she calls his parents and complains when he makes noise or comes too close to her yard.

This afternoon I saw her peeking through her window at us. She looks as if she hates everyone. Anyway, that big old house of hers is creepy."

"That big old house was once an elegant mansion," Ellen said. "It's the Windom house. Get Wanda to tell you about the Windoms sometime. They were an important family around here back in the nineteenth century."

Wishbone licked his bowl clean. "That's all right as far as it goes, but I think the real heroes of Oakdale were the guys who built the grocery stores."

"Well," Joe said, "it looks scary now. The yard's a mess. I mean, you could get lost in the grass." He ruffled Wishbone's fur. "Or at least Wishbone could."

Wishbone drew himself up. "I have an excellent sense of direction, thank you. I never get lost!"

"Maybe she needs a little help, then," Ellen said. "I don't want you to judge people too quickly, Joe. Please remember that you lost your backpack, so you need to be the one who gets it back. You do understand that, don't you?"

He nodded. "Yes, Mom. I've got to take responsibility for what I do." He paused a moment. "It's what Dad would want me to do, too."

"Yes," Ellen said with a smile. "I'll make a deal with you. You go tomorrow and ask Mrs. Grindle politely for the backpack. If she treats you badly, then I'll go and see her without you and work things out. Is that fair enough?"

"I guess so," Joe said slowly.

Later that evening when he and Wishbone were alone, Joe scratched the white-with-brown-spots dog's ears. Wishbone wriggled with pleasure. "Ah, yes, that's it! Little to the left—little more—that's the spot! You're getting right up there with Sam in the ear-scratching department. Practice that and your layups, and you'll be an expert at two things!"

"I wish we could just slip into that old place and get my backpack back," Joe said.

Wishbone gave himself a good shake. "Wouldn't work, Joe. If you got caught, they'd send you to the pound."

"Anyway, you'll go with me, won't you, fella?"

Feeling proud that Joe relied on him so much,

49

Wishbone offered his paw for Joe to shake. "You can count on me! We'll march right into the lair of the ogre, side by side!"

Hmm. March into the lair of the ogre. Just like in *Beowulf*. Beowulf thought his problems were over once he had defeated Grendel. But he was wrong! Someone held a grudge against him for killing the monster—and that grudge meant Beowulf was going to have to go to a very terrifying place and face a monster even more frightful than Grendel!

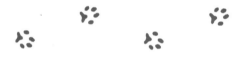

The little dog imagined himself as Beowulf, enjoying the praise of Hrothgar and his people—not even suspecting that a creature more deadly than Grendel was waiting for the chance to strike. . . .

Chapter Five

Beowulf thought that every Dane in Hrothgar's kingdom wanted to clasp his paw and speak words of gratitude for his fearless feat. He began to grow tired of standing on three legs. A bright, clear morning had come, and with it a crowd of Hrothgar's warriors. The men stood outside the damaged front door of Heorot and heard the tale of the wrestling match. Some of them found Grendel's footprints squashed deep in the soft earth. They marveled at the size of the marks. They tried putting their own feet in those prints. It was like a baby trying on a shoe made for a very big man.

Others excitedly pointed out the trail of blood leading away from Heorot. "He went running back to the swampy country of the fens, but it's too late. Oh, he's done for, all right," they said, nodding. No one mourned the passing of a monster like Grendel! Still others gazed wonderingly at the detached arm. Hrothgar had ordered his men to nail it to the wall inside the

51

doorway. It hung there as a trophy, its huge size and sharp, hooked claws providing visual proof to everyone of what a mighty and dreadful beast Grendel had been.

"I wonder if any of them would sleep in Heorot now," Wingard said to Beowulf with a grin.

Beowulf winked at him. "I suppose," he said softly, "a cat could sleep in a dog house—if he knew the dog wasn't coming back ever again!"

The celebration went on all morning. Beowulf and his warriors sat in places of honor and listened as Hrothgar's scop sang ancient songs of battle. The poet told of the hero Sigesmund, who once slew a dragon. As the scop strummed his small harp, he sang several pointed comparisons of Sigesmund to another hero— Beowulf. Everyone looked at Beowulf in awe, but this morning he made no boast. He didn't have to. He simply sat with his chin up, his eyes bright, and his tail wagging politely. He looked every inch a hero, and he knew it.

When the songs had faded away, Hrothgar stood and held up his hands for silence. "My people, let us rejoice," he said solemnly. "Grendel has done us much harm, but now the great Beowulf has paid him back, blood for blood. Beowulf, I salute you!" He raised a drinking horn high, offering a toast. "From this day on, I shall treat you as my son. You will have every gift that is in my power to give you. Now I pledge you this: Between my people and yours there will be a lasting peace. May heaven reward you, too, for you have removed a great evil from the world."

"Speech!" cried someone in the crowd.

Other voices took up the call: "Speech! Speech! Let Beowulf speak!"

"Speak, Beowulf!" Wingard said with a grin, patting his leader on the back.

Beowulf gave his friend a warning look. "Heroes don't respond to commands," he said, but his tone was good-natured. "Anyway, I'd rather face a dozen Grendels than have to make a speech. But I'll say a word or two, just to be polite." He stood and held up his paw, and everyone fell silent. Beowulf cleared his throat and began in a loud voice: "King Hrothgar, my Geats thank you for your generosity. I am pleased that my grip was great enough to give Grendel his death wound. Still, I wish I'd finished the job. Then you could have put Grendel himself up as a trophy, not just his arm! But let's hope this is a lesson for all evildoers. Let them remember that the grip of goodness is strong and that no wicked creature can escape it!" Then he bowed and sat down.

All the rest of that day was given over to feasting and rejoicing. Beowulf was presented with a great helping of venison, served to him in a dish with his name on it. He licked his chops and dug in. As for Beowulf's men, Hrothgar loaded them down with gold and jewels. Meanwhile, Hrothgar's army worked to repair the damage Grendel had caused. In his pain and terror, the monster had broken the door frame, and it had to be replaced. The iron hinges had torn completely free of the doors, too, so hard had Grendel hit them as he fled toward the swamp. Carpenters and blacksmiths worked to build a new, stronger door. Other men scrubbed away the blood.

Strangely, Beowulf could not shake a grim feeling of impending doom. Something told him that the fight was not over—yet. He could not put his paw on it, but a warrior's sixth sense kept trying to warn him to be alert. Trouble was coming from somewhere. If only he knew the direction!

Finally, just as Beowulf was beginning to fidget, Queen Wealtheow herself came and knelt before him. She held in her hands a golden mead-cup, inlaid with colorful precious stones—emeralds, sapphires, and rubies. "Take this as a gift from me, mighty warrior," she said. "You have won a great treasure by your victory over Grendel—a treasure far greater than gold and silver. For this day you have done a deed that will bring peace between the Danes and the Geats for all time. A warrior who struggles to end war is a hero indeed."

"Thank you, good queen," Beowulf said politely. "I will honor your gift always."

"Bear your gifts wisely," old Hrothgar said. "You are great in courage. Prove yourself to be great in wisdom in the years to come, Beowulf. Know that a true king is not measured by the trophies he wins or the victories he claims—but by the love his people hold for him. Be brave, but beware of being quick to anger. Hold your people's welfare at heart, not grudges against enemies. Strike only when you must defend. If you would be more than a hero—if you would be a leader of men—be always honest, be fair, and be just."

Beowulf bowed. "I will carry your words in my mind and heart, O King. You speak well."

One of Wealtheow's ladies handed her another gift, a magnificent golden collar. "Then take this, too, Beowulf," the queen proclaimed. "It was worn years ago by an ancestor of your king Hygelac. The barbarian Franks slew him and took this treasure. Then the Danes took it from the Franks in battle. Now let it return to a Geat, and may all your days be happy!"

Beowulf's eyes shone as he looked at the princely present. "I've never seen a collar so wonderful," he declared. "I will wear it with pride!"

With her own hands, the queen fastened the golden collar around the happy hero's neck. Beowulf held his head high, wishing he had a mirror.

At last, with the sun sinking low, Hrothgar ordered an end to the celebration. His men began to bring bedrolls into Heorot. However, King Hrothgar took Beowulf and his thirteen surviving Geats into the palace itself. Servants led a very sleepy Beowulf into a great room with a huge stone fireplace and piles of warm furs to sleep on. Beowulf settled gratefully on his bed, his drooping eyelids feeling heavy. The fire was nice and warm, the room toasty, and his stomach was comfortably full. He thought, *This is the life!*, as he stretched out, feeling the heat of the fire on his back fur. He yawned. *Guess I was mistaken about more trouble. Looks as if our worries are over.*

He soon fell into a deep sleep, and his dreams were wonderful ones. Dreams of victory in battle, dreams of great postwar festivities, dreams of juicy bones and of digging holes filled his head. He dreamed of chasing rabbits, of swimming in quiet pools, of running free and strong under a full moon, howling his wolfish joy.

Then suddenly, toward morning, Beowulf was jolted wide awake, for the sound of howls was real, not a dream—but there was no joy or freedom in the wails he heard. Beowulf pulled on his chain mail in a hurry. Then he ran as fast as his four legs would carry him to see what could have happened. As soon as he stepped outside, he saw a crowd of men with torches standing outside the door of Heorot. Beowulf hurried over to them.

King Hrothgar emerged from the darkness inside the great hall, his face pale in the torchlight. "Aeschere is dead!" he cried. He caught sight of Beowulf. "My friend Aeschere, my counselor and closest companion, is dead, his body taken," he said miserably.

"But . . . how?" Beowulf asked, as the crowd made a path for him. "Grendel couldn't have returned. He must be dead by now. Nothing could survive a wound as great as his."

"They say it was a different monster," the king answered.

One of the king's warriors nodded. "It was almost as big as Grendel, but thinner. Not as muscular, but more wiry, and it was a female, older than Grendel."

"It took Grendel's arm from the wall," another man added, "and . . . and it tore old Aeschere's arm off at the shoulder, as if returning wound for wound."

"An arm for an arm," the first soldier said. "That is the kind of vengeance a relative would take. We think this creature must be Grendel's mother."

Beowulf blinked, and his whiskers twitched. Monsters had mothers? Well, it made sense—though he'd never really thought about it before. What he had done to Grendel would probably have made any mother, monstrous or not, angry.

"My task is not finished, then," Beowulf announced to the assembled crowd. "Quickly, rouse my men!" He turned to Hrothgar. "Noble lord, your grief burns within my own heart. I am ashamed that the deed I promised and performed has brought this sorrow to you! Does anyone know where this new monster has gone?"

The scop, a small man, too delicately built to be a warrior, raised his hand. "Uh . . . sir, I have heard stories," he said.

Beowulf trotted over to him and put a paw on the man's knee. "Tell us," he said. "Anything might help."

The musician coughed. "Oh, I wish I could sing this," he muttered. "I'm not very good at talking. But they say that sometimes people who had to pass through the fens at night saw these creatures— Grendel and his mother, I mean. Some people saw them emerging from a deep pool of water. Others, close to the dawn, saw them going back into it again.

They say the pool is round and so deep that the water is as black as tar. Then, too, it is cold, much colder than normal lake water." The scop coughed again. "Of course, no one could be sure that the creatures they saw were really Grendel or Grendel's mother. The people were too far away to see very well. All those who have gone closer . . . well, sir, they've disappeared. Except sometimes their bones have been found, gnawed clean and white."

Hrothgar groaned.

Beowulf said kindly, "Don't mourn too much, good king. When a man is murdered, it is better that his friends set out to gain justice than that they sit weeping. My Geats and I will track this new beast into the swamps. Whether it's Grendel's brother or his mother or the ghost of Grendel himself, I promise that we'll track it down and teach it to respect a warrior's anger."

Dawn was just beginning to break in the east as the armed men set forth. Beowulf trotted ahead of them all, his nose low to the ground, sniffing out the trail. He could tell that this new monster was the same kind of creature as Grendel—but the smell was different. Disturbingly mixed with it was the coppery scent of Aeschere's blood—blood that was Beowulf's duty to avenge.

Behind Beowulf rode the men. Hrothgar, mounted on a great white horse, led the party of Geats and Danes. Beowulf hardly glanced around at them. The monster had fled through the forest, and there its trail was harder to follow, with the sharp aromas of fir boughs and pine needles masking the scent. It had left a footprint here and there in soft patches of earth, but there was nothing at all that resembled a connected trail. The men stared down in horror at the misshapen footprints. Like Grendel's, they were huge. But these prints showed long, grasping toes. The sharp marks of claws two inches long showed in the mud at the tips of the toes. Every once in a while, beside the footprints, they would spot spatters of blood. They knew it was the blood of Aeschere, the king's close friend.

The forest path proceeded downhill. All at once the trees gave way to low, reedy brush. Beowulf took a deep sniff, filling his knowing nose with the scent of mud and cold water. He detected something else, too—the cold, inhuman, froglike, snakelike scent of the monster. Beowulf narrowed his eyes and scanned the horizon. It was low and flat, with ribbons of fog winding through the landscape. The gray light of the sky reflected back from streams and puddles of standing water.

"This is the moor," King Hrothgar explained. "The land sinks away until it all becomes a boggy swamp. If the stories are right, the foul creature lives in the middle of that fen."

Beowulf said grimly, "If that's where it's gone, that is where we must go, too."

The scent became even harder to follow, washed out by the mildewy stench of the stagnant water, the rotten-egg smell of decaying swamp grass. But the monster's footprints stood out now, sunk deeply into the muddy ground. The terrible creature was taking huge strides, ten feet long.

Beowulf lowered his head and took another sniff of that dreadful mixture of smells. "We're not far behind it now."

"How do you know?" Wingard asked, his voice curious.

"The footprints are filling up as water oozes into them," the young hero explained. "But these are only half full. It would take about two hours for a footprint to fill completely with water, so we're probably about one hour behind the monster."

"Let's hurry," King Hrothgar ordered. "If it gets to the lair in the swamp, we'll never be able to get it out again. Our only hope is to catch the beast before it slips into the water."

"Follow me," Beowulf commanded. He started forward again, hating the cold, slimy feel of the mud, despising the way it sucked at his paws. But a hero had to do what a hero had to do, so he slogged on, determined and silent.

The reeds thinned out, then became widely separated clumps and tussocks. The ground transformed into oozy black mud, coated with a green scum of algae. Beowulf's pointed ears heard sounds all around. A frog scrambled to leap into a pool with a *plink!* A wading bird shrieked and took to the air with a ruffle of wings. Bubbles of foul-smelling gas rose in the puddles and popped with a *blup!* sound. The edgy men jumped at every sound, hands reaching for swords.

Only Beowulf showed no trace of fear. Nose to the ground, eyes sometimes closed in fierce concentration as he followed the sickening scent, he was lost to minor worries. All of his attention, all of his determination, was focused on the mighty monster and its mysterious destination.

Then the men came into a clearing. Before them, a great round pool opened, its waters as dark as coal. Some lump lay at the water's edge. Hrothgar gasped and dismounted. The others watched him take a few steps forward, then heard him groan.

"It's Aeschere's helmet!" the king called back in anguish. "The monster has crushed it shapeless!"

At the same moment, the water began to foam and boil. "We're too late," Wingard announced. "The creature has escaped into the water."

The surface roiled. Water snakes and strange, scaly beasts, shaped like frogs but the size of ponies, swam in the dark water. Beowulf reached for his bow, drew an arrow, and shot at a loathsome serpent. The arrow sped true and straight into the snake. It reared from the water, then fell back, dying.

Hrothgar took his hunting horn from his belt and blew a loud blast. The water monsters vanished, diving into the dark depths. The king stared at the troubled

water. "Oh, if there were some way of going after the monster!"

Beowulf shivered. The pitch-black pool was as mysterious as death itself. It promised no hope and offered no way of return. The hero swallowed hard, feeling the weight of the golden collar that the queen had fastened to his neck. "Bring me my mail shirt and my sword," he ordered in an ominous voice.

"Beowulf!" cried Wingard, his voice showing his surprise and dismay. "You can't go in after the creature. You'd never survive!"

"My mail shirt and my sword," Beowulf repeated flatly. "King Hrothgar, you said yesterday you would treat me like a son. Then treat my Geat warriors as my brothers. If I fail to come back, give them my share of the reward for killing Grendel. As for me, I will see if this water monster is made of flesh and bone. If it is, I will take revenge on it for the murder of your friend."

"Beowulf," Hrothgar warned, "you don't want to do this."

The hero had already donned his mail shirt and had fastened his sword belt into place. "No," he said softly. "No, I don't want to do this. But I have to."

Unferth stepped forward then, an expression of shame on his thin face. "You were true to your boast, Beowulf. I was wrong and you were right, and I owe you something. If . . . if you will accept it, take this magic sword," he said, offering a magnificent blade. "Its name is Hrunting. It has never failed any man who ever held it in his hands in battle."

Beowulf examined the long-hilted weapon. It was indeed well made, shining metal with mystical runic letters carved into its iron blade. "Thank you, Unferth," he said. "I will be honored to bear this sword." He slipped it into the scabbard.

Then, with a last look at his men, Beowulf took a deep breath. Inside his chest, he felt his heart pounding fast. The hero turned away and hesitated only for a moment. Then he leaped into the dark, deadly water of the fen.

Chapter Six

Beowulf was a tireless swimmer. If nothing else, he could dog-paddle for days! He kept his eyes open and held his breath as his heavy armor drew him down, down, down. He could feel the water flowing around his muzzle, making his ears flap. He could feel the pressure increasing. He could feel the fierce chill of the water. He could hear only the gurgle of bubbles and the odd roar that one heard when one's head was underwater.

He could not use his trusty nose because one deep sniff would drown him. On the edge of the fen, Beowulf had tried to appear fearless to his men and to the Danes. Once he was plummeting down through the murky, freezing water, he had to admit he felt fear. He was afraid of the unknown. Even though his skill at swimming was so great, water was not where he felt most at home. Deprived for the time being of his sense of smell and partly of his sense of hearing, Beowulf could only trust to Fate, and hope for the best.

In the bone-chilling darkness, shapes swam past him. Some of them were long and twisting, others squat and ugly. They were the water monsters, sea dragons and serpents, Beowulf realized. He gripped the hilt of Hrunting, his unfailing sword, tight in his teeth and struck at them when they tried to approach. Some he wounded, and others he frightened off. When they had all gone, Beowulf replaced Hrunting in its scabbard and used his legs to swim even deeper into the water. His chest ached and began to burn. How long had he been descending? It seemed like a whole day!

Then, before he knew it, he struck the bottom, his four paws sinking deep into thick muck. Something seized him from behind and dragged him. Faintly through the water he could hear long, sharp nails scratching and scrabbling against the gold collar that he wore—but it was well made; it was not just a decoration, but a fine piece of armor as well. Beowulf's attacker could not choke him as long as he had the rigid, protective collar around his neck. But he couldn't draw his sword or even turn enough to strike back at the creature confronting him. He felt his enemy lug him along, his hind legs trailing through the gloppy, freezing mud.

Finally—he blinked water from his eyes—he found himself in a dry place. Well, it was dry compared to the fen, anyway. A smoky red fire burned and crackled in a stone fireplace. Overhead, from a tall, rounded ceiling, stalactites of orange-red stone jutted down toward him. It was a cave—a cave that held air.

Beowulf gasped and panted, frantically filling his aching lungs.

The cave air smelled terrible, like rotting fish and decayed pond weed, but it was air. Beowulf made a desperate twist, pulling himself free of the deadly grasp that had held him. He felt the bony fingers lose their grip on his golden collar, and at last he jerked away. Turning, he almost barked in alarm.

It was another creature like Grendel, but an old female. Her huge head was completely bald and covered with scales. Her face was wide, like a frog's, and a dirty green. Huge warts and lumps sprouted on her low forehead and covered both cheeks. Her ears were like fans, ragged and torn as though from years of fighting. The neck that supported her head was crooked and bony, like a goose's neck. The shoulders were broad and muscular, and the arms were thin and stringy with sinews as powerful as rawhide thongs. She wore a leathery, togalike dress made of fish skins sewn together. The creature's mouth was open. It drooled a thin green string of spittle, and its long, pointed, yellow teeth gnashed back and forth. The monster hissed at Beowulf. It had to be Grendel's mother. He had to back away. Her breath was so bad that he thought it might be poisonous.

"You took your revenge against the wrong one, monster," Beowulf said grimly. "Aeschere didn't defeat your son. I did! But not before your little monster killed one of my men." He drew his sword and prepared for battle.

If the monstrous creature could understand him, she gave no sign of it. Her eyes, yellow with slitted irises, like those of a snake, narrowed. She lunged at Beowulf, her long arms reaching, her cruel claws clutching.

"I don't think so!" Beowulf danced away, light on his four paws, the sword balanced in his mouth. The ogre towered over him, but he thought if he could only get an opening, he could end the fight soon enough. Fortunately, he hadn't boasted that he would use no sword on Grendel's mother!

She circled him like a lynx, one of those wildcats of the northern mountains. A snarling growl bubbled up from deep in her throat. Beowulf turned, keeping his sharp eyes on her, watching for an opening. As he did, he saw a huge crumpled heap in the corner near the fireplace. It was Grendel, stone-cold dead on the floor. So the monster had made it home before he perished! That explained how Grendel's mother knew just where to go when she sought revenge.

Beowulf had turned in almost a complete circle. Now he stood on the edge of a round, water-filled hole in the floor, the opening into this cave. The mud underfoot was slippery and treacherous. As if Grendel's mother knew this, she suddenly pounced.

However, the hero was ready. With all his might, the sword hilt gripped tightly in his teeth, Beowulf swung Hrunting in a whistling arc. The blade struck the ogre smack on the skull—and bounced off, ringing like a bell. Grendel's mother jerked away, grinning and hissing. Her bald head showed no sign of a wound.

Impossible! Hrunting was a very strong, sharp blade. . . .

The creature was laughing at Beowulf! In a gargling, hissing, bubbly voice, she spat, "Foolis-s-shh mortal! My life has-s-s been charmed! No s-s-s-sword made by human hands-s-s can hurt me." From her side she drew a wicked weapon, a short, curved sword with an age-blackened blade. It had been made so that it had teeth, like a saw blade. In the monster's enormous taloned hand, the sword looked no bigger than a knife—but it looked sharp enough to kill.

She thrust at him, and Beowulf struck at the sword with Hrunting. The two blades clashed and clanged together, and sparks flew.

"Is-s-s your life ch-charmed, too?" Grendel's mother hissed. "I th-think not, s-s-small hero! Thank you for telling me the name of my victim. I thought I had killed King Hrothgar—I chos-s-se the oldes-s-st man there. Now you have s-s-shown me that I was-s-s mis-s-staken and mus-s-st return. Firs-s-st, though, I s-s-shall have you for s-s-supper!"

Angry, Beowulf dropped the useless sword. "Think again," he said. "My mother didn't raise me to be the main course for a monster!"

With a wild cry, Grendel's mother leaped on him. Her weight carried Beowulf to the floor, his legs flailing. He saw the curved blade slash down, and he felt it hit his chest. . . .

Clang! The monster's sword scraped against the finely crafted mail shirt that Beowulf wore. It had been made by master smiths, men who had been taught their craft by the great Wayland Smith himself, the legendary workman whom some thought had been a god in disguise.

The ogre screamed in frustration and drew back for another blow, but Beowulf was faster. He rolled over, got his feet beneath him, and dashed away.

Grendel's mother hurled the sword at him. Yipe! It came spinning just over his ears, brushing their fur. Beowulf ducked in the nick of time. He turned to face her, only to find that she was leaping toward him. They hit the floor in a tangle of arms and legs. That foul breath blasted in Beowulf's face again, and he felt the monster tighten her grip on him. She grunted with effort, and Beowulf gasped. Her arms were like the tentacles of a giant octopus—she was trying to crush the life out of him! He frantically tried to twist and wriggle enough to seize one of her arms in his mouth. Her son must have warned her about the warrior's mighty grip. She let out a scornful, hissing laugh.

Everything was going dark. The crushing arms were squeezing him so tight that Beowulf couldn't breathe, let alone move. Desperately, he tried to roll. Grendel's mother, intent on choking him, rolled along with him. She did not notice what the hero was trying to do. Then, with a frantic heave, Beowulf poured every ounce of strength he had into shoving her to the left— and suddenly he had heaved her into the fireplace!

She screeched and leaped, letting go her hold. Beowulf darted away from her. The monster was smoldering, and she quickly jumped into the round pool of water. There came a loud hissing noise, and steam billowed up.

Desperately, Beowulf looked around. Then he noticed something he hadn't seen before. Above the fireplace was a rough stone mantel, and hanging just above it was a sword. But not just any sword. This one was huge, as long as a man was tall, with a jeweled hilt and a broad blade shining like silver. The blade bore engraved runes, the letters of the Scandinavian languages, and Beowulf read them: GIANTS MADE ME.

Giants! What had the monster said? No sword made by humans could hurt her. But what about a sword made by giants?

There was no time to think. Grendel's mother was already clambering out of the water, snarling. Beowulf scrambled up the crumpled body of Grendel, leaped from there to a table, scampered from there to a shelf, then made the broad jump of his life. His front paws caught on the mantel, his hind legs kicking for balance. He heard Grendel's mother screech at him.

Somehow or other, he managed to raise one hind paw up on the mantel and pulled himself up. He snatched the hilt of the sword in his mighty jaw. The monster was running toward him, her claws stretching out to tear at him. Beowulf launched himself through the air, spinning. He swung the giant-forged sword around with all his might!

Chunch! The blade bit into something. Beowulf struck the stone floor, hard. The sword flew from his jaw as the breath rushed out of his body. He heard something heavy fall.

Dizzily, he got to his feet. He could hardly believe what he saw.

His stroke had hit that gooseneck of hers. With one clean blow, the sword had cut the monster's head off. The body toppled to the floor and lay dead.

The air stank of white-hot steel. Beowulf saw the giant's sword across from him. As he watched, the blade, covered with the monster's blood, dissolved like ice on a hot day, white vapors streaming from it. "I've heard of people having hot blood," he muttered, "but never anything like this!"

He wearily retrieved Hrunting. Then he picked up the hilt of the giant's sword. Finally, he took several deep breaths and plunged into the cold water once more.

This time no monsters bothered him as he swam. He thought grimly that they could sense that he had bested the two fiercest beasts around and they didn't want to tangle with him. His chest began to ache, but above he could see the glimmering light of day. Swimming harder and harder, he pulled himself upward toward the light.

After what seemed like hours, his head broke the surface and he gasped, gulping in air. He was so tired that he started to sink, but then someone clasped his paw.

"Hold on!" It was the welcome voice of Wingard.

Beowulf went limp, letting his friend haul him to the shore, and to safety.

For a few moments he could only lie on his stomach, his fur soaking wet and covered with sludge. He coughed up water and panted. Then he raised his muzzle and took a few sniffs. "Where is everyone?"

"They thought you were dead," Wingard explained. "You were under the water for so long."

"But you waited."

Wingard shrugged. "I swore to be faithful to you, my lord."

"You shall be rewarded." Beowulf was exhausted. He got to his feet and stood trembling. "Hang this bag over your saddle, my friend. Then, if you don't mind, I'll ride back to Heorot behind you."

"What's in the bag?" Wingard asked.

"I will tell you later," Beowulf said. "For now, know this—we return to celebrate another victory. Ready to party, Wingard?"

"Always ready, my lord," Wingard answered with a grin.

"Good! Let's hope that Hrothgar has some more of that delicious venison left. If I've learned nothing else on this trip, I've discovered that battling monsters gives one a tremendous appetite."

"No!" Wingard said, pretending to be surprised.

Beowulf grinned. "Okay, okay, I know what you're thinking. Digging a hole gives me a tremendous appetite. Taking a nap gives me a tremendous appetite.

Having a snack gives me a tremendous appetite! But, hey, I'm a hero, right? So let's go to Heorot and see if we can scare up a hero sandwich!"

Beowulf got his feast. The Danes were both surprised and happy to see that he was still alive, and they doubled the presents they had already given him. For days, it seemed that all Beowulf could do was tell and retell the story of his two great fights.

The evenings were spent at banquets and parties. At long last the Danes slept in Heorot without fear and in safety. Hrothgar himself slept there the first night after Beowulf's return.

Finally, the time came when Beowulf and his men had to depart for home. The cheering Danes saw them off. When he returned to Geat-Land, Beowulf found he had to tell the whole story over again, until he began to feel like a dog who got hold of an elephant bone. In other words, it was too much of a good thing!

Still, Beowulf's king, Hygelac, was very impressed and gave Beowulf and his men still more treasures. Beowulf woke up one morning to find that he was famous—a scop was singing a song all about his two terrible battles. Beowulf thought he had reached the height of his career.

How wrong he was. . . .

Chapter Seven

In the warm sunlight of Saturday morning, Joe gazed uneasily at the old Victorian mansion. It seemed to be empty and deserted, but it was hard to tell for sure. "Are you *positive* she's not at home?" he asked Sean warily.

"I'm sure," Sean said. "She drove away in her antique car about five minutes before you got here."

Wishbone wanted to be out enjoying this great Saturday, which was warm and dry and sunny after all the rain. Instead, there he sat beside Joe's feet, sensing his friend's uneasiness growing by the second. He looked up hopefully. "Well, she's not at home, so you'll have to come up with another plan. I know—you can go home and feed the dog!"

"I have to get my books back," Joe said.

Wishbone sighed. "Something told me you were going to say that." Actually, he had to admit Joe was right. Wishbone was a dog who had the greatest respect for education.

Sean said, "Maybe it's good that she went off grocery shopping. While she's away, you could sneak over and take a look around."

"I can't do that when she's not at home," Joe objected.

Sean smiled. "That's just the point. With Mrs. Grindle, it's better to look around when she's *not* there."

"Come on," Joe said uneasily. He gripped two of the fence pickets in his hands and tugged at them as he looked at the house. He wasn't trying to pull them down. Wishbone could sense that Joe was just nervous and didn't know what to do with his hands—a problem dogs never had. Joe looked around at Sean. "She can't be as bad as you claim she is."

"You don't know her," Sean answered quickly. "She's *strange*, Joe. Sort of a hermit. I mean, she never talks to anyone, she never smiles at anyone—she hardly ever goes out, except when she has to go buy groceries. She's pretty weird, and I told you how she's been so mean to me."

"Did she call your mom and complain about our playing ball?" Joe asked.

Sean shook his head. "No. She's called lots of times before, though."

"Well, I can't go inside her house when she's not at home," Joe said, letting go of the fence and dusting the powdery white paint off his hands. "That would be . . . like being a burglar or something."

Wishbone nodded his agreement. "Uh-huh.

You're right, Joe. You'd be like a cat burglar. Though, come to think of it, I wonder why they're called that. No thief in his right mind would ever think to go around stealing cats!"

Joe crossed his arms as he stood beside the fence, still looking up the grassy, overgrown hill at the old house. Sean stood next to him, thoughtfully bouncing a basketball from time to time. "I've got an idea, Joe. You don't exactly have to go *inside* the house, you know. I mean, if Mrs. Grindle took the backpack off the fence, she probably just put it up on her back porch. It's screened in, but you could look in through the screen if you got close enough."

"I don't know," Joe said hesitantly.

"Come on," Sean told him. "At least if it's there, you'll know what happened to it."

Joe looked at Sean suspiciously. "The next thing you'll say is that since it's mine, it wouldn't hurt to grab it and run off with it. No, thanks. Anyway, I don't think it's right to go into her yard when she's not at home."

Sean bounced the basketball. "But you wouldn't have known she wasn't at home if I hadn't told you. And you would have gone up and rung her bell then, right? Anyway, what's the big deal? If we were selling school candy or something, we'd have to go up to her house. I mean, there's nothing illegal about just going up and knocking on her door or ringing her bell. While you're there, you can always take one quick look around. Joe, I would never advise you to take something off her porch. That's wrong, but just look-ing—how is that going to hurt anyone?"

"I guess it won't." Joe took a deep breath. "Okay, come with me."

Wishbone jumped up. "Joe! No! Bad idea, Joe!" The concerned dog ran after the boys as they walked down the sidewalk. Joe opened Mrs. Grindle's gate, hesitated for a moment, then started through.

Wishbone barked sharply, then leaped forward and tugged at Joe's jeans leg.

Joe frowned down at him. "What's wrong, boy— Wow!"

Joe lurched backward and slammed the gate shut just as a gray-white blur came tearing around the back of the house, barking and growling. A bulldog slammed against the gate, crashing into it so hard that the wood rattled.

Sean leaped back with a yelp. "Oh, man, I thought he'd be inside, or at least shut up on the back porch! He's almost never outside!"

The bulldog was jumping up as if he wanted to scramble over the fence and pounce on the boys. He was barking at the top of his lungs, low-pitched snarls that were enough to frighten any puppy out of a year's growth.

"Let's get out of here!" Joe yelled.

He, Sean, and Wishbone raced back up the side-walk to Sean's yard, the bulldog in hot pursuit of them on the other side of the picket fence.

Wishbone was panting. He looked up at Joe. "I

told you it was a bad idea. I knew there was a dog in there!"

Joe gasped and sat down on the driveway, his back against the garage. "You knew there was a dog in there!" he said angrily to Sean.

Wishbone stared at his best friend. "I just said that!"

"Why didn't you tell me?" Joe asked hotly, and Wishbone realized that Joe was talking to Sean.

"Sorry, Joe," Sean apologized. "Really, he's usually outside only at night. I think he spends most of the day hanging out in the house, or sometimes sleeping on the back porch. Man, would you just look at the size of him!"

The bulldog was peering through the fence at them. He had a wide, boxy, punched-in face, and he snuffled and grumbled as he danced from side to side. His lower eyelids drooped, showing circles of pink beneath his bloodshot brown eyes. He was big, even for an English bulldog—at least knee-high to Joe. Wishbone wondered what it would be like to tangle with him. It certainly wouldn't be pleasant!

"Maybe your dog got him upset," Sean suggested. "He barked."

Joe leaned over to scratch Wishbone's head. "He was trying to warn us. He probably smelled the bulldog."

Wishbone tilted his head. "A little lower, thanks. Good grief, couldn't *you* smell him? Someday I'll have to have a long talk with you about how to use your nose, Joe."

The bulldog had stopped its barking, but continued to stare at them. Its big floppy jowls gave the dog's mouth a permanent frown, and its pointed, yellowish teeth showed over its glistening black lips. Now and then it rumbled softly, as if it were building up to a roar.

"I guess you have to wait for Mrs. Grindle to come back, huh?" Sean asked. He had slumped next to Joe, but then he got up again.

"I guess we do," Joe agreed, getting to his feet.

Settling down, Wishbone scratched his left ear thoughtfully. "I think you're right, Joe. Ordinarily, I'd suggest a heroic confrontation. Mano a mano combat. Or, in my case, doggo a doggo. But that monster might go for you, not me—and I don't want you to get hurt."

Sean turned and tossed the basketball at the basket. It missed completely, bounced off the backstop, and Joe caught it. "Not shaken up, are you?"

"Yeah, I guess I am, a little," Sean admitted. "See, Dad told me never to bother Mrs. Grindle. I mean, he told me that, like the first *day* we moved here. Just the idea of talking to her gives me a case of the goose bumps. Seriously."

"I don't want to talk to her, either," Joe confessed. "But I have to."

"Maybe we could trap the bulldog or something—" Sean began.

Joe gave him a look.

With a weak smile, Sean shrugged. "Sorry. It was just an idea."

Wishbone sniffed. "Not a good one, though. It probably would take a shark cage to keep you safe from him!"

"Let's just wait, okay?" Joe suggested. He tossed the ball and made a basket.

"Hey!" Sean said. "Two points."

"Yea," Joe said. It wasn't really a cheer. It was more like the noise someone might make if he had just been told he had to do something he disliked doing. Joe picked up the ball. "Might as well do a few free throws," he said. "We can worry about Mrs. Grindle when she comes home."

"You do the free throws." Wishbone flopped down on the pavement, feeling the warm concrete against his tummy, and stared at the bulldog, who continued to follow the movements of the boys through the fence. "I'll stand guard. If that beast tries to break through, I'll sound the alarm and hold him off!"

Joe and Sean took turns shooting baskets. Wishbone wondered what might have happened if Joe had actually gone into Mrs. Grindle's yard. Nothing good, probably.

Hmm, this reminds me of the last part of *Beowulf*. Joe might have ended up like the escaping slave who went where he wasn't supposed to go. I mean, this guy was just looking for a place to hide, and he crept into a cave. Inside the cave he found... treasure! A big pile of gold, silver, pearls, emeralds, rubies . . . and kibble!

He thought that if he could give the treasure to his master, maybe he would be set free and not have to be a slave anymore. Of course, he couldn't carry that whole cave full of treasure out by himself.

So he took just one item—a gleaming golden cup. Oh, it was beautiful, all right. It was a priceless work of art.

Unfortunately, the poor man didn't have any idea of who—or, rather, of *what*—owned the cup!

In the warm sun, Wishbone began once more to fantasize about Beowulf—an older Beowulf this time, a great leader who had risen to become king of the Geats. He found himself, late in life, facing one last deadly enemy.

Chapter Eight

You'd think that Beowulf would have been set for life when he became a hero, but for heroes and everyone else, life went on. After Beowulf's great battles with Grendel and Grendel's mother, years passed and change came. The king of the Geats, Hygelac, died in combat. His son, Heardred, was too young to become king, and for several years Beowulf ruled in his place.

After Heardred grew up and claimed the throne, Beowulf once again became a leader of warriors. King Heardred led the Geats into war against the Swedes, and many murderous battles took their toll. Most of Beowulf's fighting men, including Wingard, his best friend, died in that terrible fighting. At last the Swedes killed Heardred, too, leaving the Geats without a leader.

Once more they turned to Beowulf, and he became their king. He led them to victory over the Swedes, but then he took them down a whole new path. The Geats made peace with their neighbors, and warfare ended. For fifty good years, Beowulf led the Geats well, growing old and watching the world change. After all that time, his last enemy appeared, deadly and evil. . . .

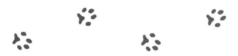

Feeling his age, King Beowulf sat on his throne in the palace of the Geats. He was grayer than he had been, and his movements were stiffer. Some mornings he had to stretch a long time before his hind legs and tail felt strong. He had become lonely over the years, with so many of his friends snatched by Fate, passing from this world in battles or shipwrecks, or taken from it by disease and age. Still, even though Beowulf had become old, he was a handsome and noble king, and his people treated him with love and respect.

Now one of his thanes—Beowulf sometimes had trouble, these days, remembering their names—stood before him, guarding a miserable-looking captive, a skinny blond man dressed in muddy gray-and-black rags and carrying a small bundle wrapped in old, torn cloth. The prisoner stared glumly at the floor, his long hair hanging down on either side of his face. He was dirty, and five days' growth of beard bristled on his chin.

"This is the hall of justice," Beowulf told the man. "My thane has brought you to me so I may hear your case and pass judgment. He says that you are a renegade, a servant running away from his master. Tell me your name."

"I am Feodred of the Frisians," the man mumbled.

The king nodded. "Very well, Feodred the Frisian. What is your story?"

The prisoner muttered something, and a guard prodded him with the butt of his spear. "Stand up straight! Speak up for the king," the guard ordered.

"I ran away," Feodred said, speaking louder this time. He looked up, glaring. "Even a slave should be protected from bullies and tyrants."

Beowulf almost growled in his anger. "Slave? I don't permit my people to own slaves," he proclaimed.

"But some do, sir," the thane told him. "It's the old way, you see. You capture a man in battle, and he becomes your slave. It was our custom for generations, and a few warriors—just some of them—think that taking slaves is their right."

Beowulf sniffed. His nose was as keen as ever, and he could smell the thane's nervousness. It didn't take the old king two guesses to realize that this man was one of those warriors who believed owning slaves was a right. "They think they have a right to disobey an order given by their king, do they? We will simply have to teach them differently, then," he said, staring hard at the warrior, who shuffled his feet and coughed.

Beowulf paused, trying to identify another elusive odor—a bitter, scorched smell. He could not place it, and after a moment he spoke to the prisoner in a milder voice. "No harm will come to you, Feodred. How did you come to be a slave?"

"I was born in Friesland," the prisoner said. "Since I was twelve years old, I have been a sailor. Last year I was with the crew of a vessel that tried to take one of your ships. A warrior captured me in the sea battle, and I have been his slave ever since. But trying to fight the Geat ship wasn't my idea."

"If what you say is true, you will be set free," Beowulf assured him. "Is that all?"

"No, sir." Feodred unwrapped his package. The torn, dirty rag dropped away, and everyone in the room gasped. The captive held a marvelous golden cup, turning it left and right so that it gleamed in the torchlight. The cup was intricately cast, with figures of gods and ships wrought on its surface: Thor the Thunderer was there, brandishing his hammer. Beside him was Odin the One-Eyed, king of all the gods, who had given up his right eye so that he might learn what the future held. A row of shimmering pearls circled the outer rim of the cup, and red rubies winked from its base. Gazing at the masterpiece of craftsmanship, Beowulf could not help but think of the cup that Queen Wealtheow of the Danes had given him at the celebration all those years ago. The treasure offered by the prisoner was almost as precious and wonderful as Beowulf's cup—surely it had been made for a great king.

"Where did you get this?" Beowulf asked, pushing himself up with his front paws.

"He stole it from his master, of course!" cried the thane whose men had captured the runaway. "They're all like that, all these sneaking, sniveling slaves! Thieves, every one of them."

"No!" Feodred looked wildly from the thane to Beowulf. "No, King Beowulf, I swear I did not! I . . . I found this cup. And, sir, I . . . found a great treasure besides, all buried in the earth."

Beowulf settled back on his throne, twitching his

tail to a more comfortable position. "I think you'd better explain. You don't just go to bury a bone and dig up a pile of gold!"

The man gave a weak smile. "I didn't dig at all, Your Majesty. As I fled from my master, I heard his dogs baying, hot on my trail. Hoping to hide from them, I found a cave in the rocks—a very narrow cave. I crept inside, into the darkness. I groped deeper and deeper into the earth, unable to see. Then I felt the walls open around me. The air caused me to feel as if I were in some great open space. Loose pieces of metal covered the floor. The least sound I made came back to me seconds later as an echo. I struck a light. I saw that I had stumbled into some great treasure barrow."

Beowulf cocked his head, his ears perking up. "A pagan tomb? I have heard of such things."

"I don't know what it was," Feodred admitted. He looked around. "The cave was larger than this room, though. Gold and jewels were strewn everywhere. They rose to a great heap in the middle of the floor, a mound taller than my head. I saw piles of coins, old decayed leather bags spilling out green emeralds and blue sapphires, bars of gold and silver, and wonderful weapons."

The old king felt his heart beat a little faster. Despite all the years of peace, Beowulf had a warrior's heart, and he dearly loved a well-made sword, pike, or spear. Unconsciously wagging his tail a little, he said, "Describe them for me. Tell me about these wonderful weapons."

Feodred closed his eyes, as if seeing the cave again in memory. "My lord, I saw swords sheathed in pure gold and daggers with bright silver blades. I even found a broad axe whose long wooden handle was inlaid with agate, opal, amethyst, and beryl. I saw bows tipped with fine sea ivory, jeweled spears, arrows with ebony shafts, peacock feathers, and heads made from pure silver. I stood among hundreds of these weapons, thousands—enough to equip a whole army of heroes."

"Hmm," Beowulf murmured, licking his chops. "It sounds wonderful, indeed. No wonder someone was smart enough to dig a deep hole and bury it!"

Feodred swallowed. "When I saw all that treasure, I knew that I might use it to buy my freedom. But my master had been harsh with me—if I simply returned and told him I knew where the hoard was, how did I know that he would believe me? I decided I would take just one princely piece with me. It would prove that I had found this magnificent treasure house. I settled on this beautiful jeweled cup. When hours had passed and night had come, I slipped back the way I had come. By then my master and his dogs had passed by without finding me. I was on my way back to my master's house when your thane and his men came across me and arrested me." The prisoner blinked fearfully at the thane standing beside him.

The king lowered his head. "Come here, Feodred. You don't have to be afraid now." The slave nervously took two steps toward the throne. Beowulf stood up.

"Put the cup down beside my throne. Now hold out your hand."

When the prisoner did so, Beowulf put his paw in the man's hand.

"I pledge you my word, miserable captive, that from this day, you are free. I will give you gold enough to keep you comfortable. You may sail home to Friesland on the first of our ships bound that way. Any man of the Geats who injures you or tries to take your freedom will have to answer to me. That should be enough. My people know that my anger is worse than my bark!"

The grateful Feodred began to blurt out his thanks, but at that same moment the hall doors flew open with a crash. A frightened young soldier darted inside, his eyes terrified beneath the protective bronze visor of his horned helmet. "My lord!" he called in a panicky voice. "My lord!"

Beowulf looked up sharply. "What is it, soldier? Have enemy ships stormed the beach? Are we being invaded?"

The cluster of men near the throne spread out, making way for the soldier to stumble closer to the king. The warrior was clearly exhausted. His mail shirt and shield were both stained with soot, his face streaked with sweat. He was gasping for breath, as if he had run a long way. The strange scorched smell that Feodred carried, but stronger, a terrible stench, clung to the soldier. "It's worse, my king! A monster has burned our village!"

Beowulf's head snapped up sharply, his fur bristling. "What! What kind of monster?"

The frightened warrior gestured frantically, sweeping his hands apart to indicate something enormous. "A flying dragon, a gruesome winged creature, my lord! It came in the night, a shape dark against the stars. We heard the clamor of its wings, like the sound a ship's sails make when the wind first cracks into them. Men gazed up into the darkness, wondering what strange bird could be flying beneath the stars. Then it dived from the sky, opening its mouth and breathing out white-hot jets of poisonous flames!" The young man began to sob and tremble.

"Calm yourself," Beowulf said kindly. "That's a good boy. Now tell us what happened next."

With terror in his eyes, the soldier stammered, "It came again and again, darting down, spewing death, then soaring off into the night. I saw the fiery flames from its mouth leap out, striking the houses. They burst into fire at once, giving the people sleeping inside no chance to escape. I heard their screams. . ." He covered his face with his hands.

"We must arm ourselves at once!" shouted the thane.

Beowulf raised a paw. "Not until we know what we are facing! Did you clearly see this creature, or was it only a dark shape in the night?"

The soldier lowered his hands. "I saw it, my lord, in the light of the burning village. It was long, like a serpent, but it had talons, too, huge hooked claws. Its scales glimmered green in the light of the flaming houses. At the end of the long snaky neck was a great head. It was far larger than a horse's head, with a gaping mouth filled with deadly, curved white teeth, as long and sharp as deadly daggers. When the people ran from the fire, the dragon alighted and caught three of them. One was my captain; the other two people were from the town, a man and a woman. The monster—it played with them, wounding them and then letting them hobble a little way before snatching at them again with its gruesome claws. It played with them the way a cat plays with a wounded mouse!"

Beowulf felt the fur bristle on his neck and shoulders. "I never heard of anything so terrible!"

"Worse followed, my king. Finally, tiring of its play, the dragon breathed fire on its helpless victims. Then with three great gulps it swallowed them, one after the other."

"Where was this?"

"The village was Barrow-Town, my king. It *was,* for it exists no more." The young man lowered his head. "My duty was to guard the town. No one needs to guard it now, for only a pathetic pile of ash remains. That is the sad news I came to tell you, my lord. Barrow-Town no longer stands where it has stood for years."

"On the eastern shore, my lord," the thane told Beowulf. "It's near the rocky headland that looks out over the sea, not very far from where my men found this runaway."

Beowulf sat back on his throne. His nose twitched. The soldier had brought in with him a poisonous smell, a sickening stench of flame and venom. "A dragon's treasure," the old king said slowly, turning to the man who had discovered the golden cup. "That is what you found under the earth, friend Feodred. It was the treasure hoard of a dragon."

"We should put this man to death!" the thane snarled, and he drew his sword. "He brought this bane upon us!"

Beowulf bared his teeth. "No! Put away your sword this instant! Have I not given my word? How was this man to know that what he took was from the treasure mound of a dragon?"

An aged man with a bald head and a long white beard stepped forward. He was one of Beowulf's counselors, a man known for his learning, and he stooped to speak to the king. "My lord, there are old stories about a dragon that once lived in the countryside near Barrow-Town. Legends do say that in the dim past, a tribe of warlike people settled on the headland there. In many battles they gathered great heaps of gold. But Fate willed that they all die, all but one—the guardian of the treasure. Old tales say that this man found a cavern in a hillside overlooking the ocean. There he brought the treasures of his people and hid them away. Afterward, he sang a song of sorrow for his people."

The old man cleared his throat, and in a quavering, high-pitched voice, he sang:

Hold, Earth, what the heroes cannot,
Take these treasures! True men
First dug the fair ore from you!
Where have they gone, the gatherers of gold?
Their silver-strung harps now stand silent,
Their falcons fly no more afield.
No stallion of theirs strikes sparks from the stones,
Cruel death has claimed my kith and my kin.

When the old man had finished, Beowulf said, "A sad lament."

"The story goes on," the old counselor said. "The last survivor wandered the world until Death found him, too, and gathered him to his people. No one could discover the hidden entrance to the cavern, though memories of it caused men to name the next settlement made nearby 'Barrow-Town.' Yet even before the town was begun, so legends claim, the old dragon found the hoard and crept into the cave. A dragon's dark spirit delights in gold, they say. There beneath the earth this great flying serpent found gold enough for a flight of dragons."

Beowulf tilted his head, thinking. "And dragons sleep on gold," he said slowly.

"On it—or burrowed down beneath it," the old counselor replied. "Likely while Feodred here was rummaging through the golden treasures, the hibernating dragon lay there all along, asleep under the pilfered pile."

The recently freed prisoner looked pale and sick.

Thoughtfully, Beowulf scratched his chin with his left hind paw. "All this—the first time the dragon came—how long ago was it?"

"A century or more before the time of the Geats, my lord," the counselor advised Beowulf. "If the old tales have any truth, the dragon has slept undisturbed for three hundred years. But now, as we hear, the foul creature is awake again. A dragon's heart is hungry for gold, and a dragon numbers to the last ounce how much treasure he has. Now the beast will feed his anger and his belly. He will feast on the Geats! This monster will never rest until he recovers his stolen cup—or until he is killed."

Beowulf blinked. A dragon could go for three hundred years without so much as a snack? What a repulsive and unnatural creature it must be! Aloud, the king proclaimed, "Let the dragon be killed, then. No dragon made that cup, nor did any of his scaly kind create the ravishing riches and wonderful weapons in that barrow. They are the work of mortal men! Let my Geats take the treasure trove. Let it be in the hands of men once more." Rising stiffly from his throne, the old king leaped to the floor. His four aged legs were no longer those of a fine young chieftain, but they bore him up sturdily. "Call my best warriors together," he ordered. "Let us end this dragon's curse before sundown tomorrow. Either the dragon must die, or I must. May Fate be kind to the Geats."

Today, he thought, *may I have just a portion of*

my old strength and cunning. It's plain that I'll need them both!

The old king knew he was in for a life-or-death struggle. He even felt a little fear. Still, heroism is all about mastering fear, and so he prepared to show himself a hero once more—just as Joe and I prepared to face the unknown!

Chapter Nine

"Uh-oh," Sean said, tapping Joe on the shoulder and pointing toward the street. "Here she comes."

Wishbone and Joe both turned to look. Joe had been poised with the basketball in both hands, ready to try another free throw, and Wishbone was sitting on the driveway behind him. The Jack Russell terrier blinked in surprise when he saw the vehicle that was cruising slowly and majestically down the street. "Wow! If I were the kind of dog who chased cars, that looks like one I could catch!"

"You weren't kidding, Sean. She *does* drive an old car," Joe said, a touch of awe in his voice.

The two-toned auto was a 1955 Chevrolet hardtop, yellow body with a green roof, and it rolled down the street at a sedate speed of about fifteen miles per hour.

Sean nodded. "I think she's too stingy to buy new wheels. Of course, she hardly ever drives—usually just to get groceries and back—so maybe she doesn't think she needs a new car."

Joe shook his head and in an admiring voice said, "Maybe she doesn't. It looks like she keeps this one in great condition."

It was true. The cheerful morning sun gleamed on the rounded fenders and mirrorlike chrome bumpers of the big old-fashioned car. It was spotless, and its engine hummed along quietly. Behind the picket fence, the bulldog had collapsed onto his stomach. He lay breathing hard through his nose with an assortment of snorts and whistles. His stubby ears pricked up at the sound of the car, and he got to his feet.

Joe, Sean, and Wishbone watched as the Chevrolet turned the corner. "Her garage is behind the house," Sean explained, pointing toward a grove of tall, dark green cedars in the backyard of Mrs. Grindle's house. "You can't see it from here because of the trees, but the driveway is off Oak Street."

"Well," Joe said, handing the basketball to Sean, "I guess I'd better get over there." He hesitated for just a second, then added, "Want to come with me?"

With a sickly grin, Sean shook his head. "No, not really."

"Okay," Joe said.

Sean squirmed. "Look, my folks have yelled at me so many times for bothering her that I don't want to risk it. I'm really sorry, Joe, but I'm afraid of her."

"I know you are," Joe replied. "It's okay, really. You probably have something else to do, anyway."

Sean was blushing from embarrassment and shame. "Uh . . . I sort of promised Mom I'd mow the lawn. Guess I'd better get started on that. Good luck, though."

Wishbone looked up at Joe in a reassuring way. "Don't worry. I'll be with you all the way! A dog and his boy, courageous and bold to the end. You can count on me anytime!" Just then the bulldog jerked its head around sharply at the sound of a gate opening. The heavy gray dog barked, a deep, resounding bark, then dashed off around the corner of the house.

Joe went to the fence and looked up the hill. Following his gaze, Wishbone could just see a corner of the screened-in back porch of the old house. He heard the door squeak open, and a moment later he saw the bulldog safely behind the screen. A shadowy figure of a woman holding a couple of grocery bags—Mrs. Grindle, no doubt—appeared just for a moment behind the bulldog and then disappeared into the house.

"Looks like the bulldog is locked up," Joe mumbled. He sighed and straightened his shoulders. "I really hate this, but we'd better get it over with. Come on, fella."

Wishbone trotted along beside Joe. "Come on, Joe. You have to be brave! Don't think of that enormous animal with the razor-sharp teeth. Don't think of how nasty that old woman might be. Don't think of how spooky that old house looks." He glanced up. "I hope this pep talk is making you feel braver. Somehow it's not doing much for me!"

They paused at the front gate. Joe gazed over it, and Wishbone got close enough to stare between two of the slats.

Beyond the gate lay the shaggy front yard. Once it had probably been planted with a bright bed of flowers, surrounded by greenery, but now the rosebushes grew wild and unpruned. The ragged grass was at least three weeks overdue for mowing. A path of dark gray flagstones led from the gate up to the wooden steps of the front porch. Looking at the place, Wishbone couldn't help but think that the house didn't look or smell scary . . . well, not exactly. *It was a lot worse yesterday, when everything was damp and moldy. Today the sun's shining on it, and it's really a handsome house. It just needs a dab of paint or two.*

Wishbone took a deep sniff. Hmm—damp earth, lots of grass and growing things, car smells, and the bulldog. But the bulldog didn't smell like an immediate problem. Wishbone's educated nose told him that the other dog wasn't close—he was still behind the screen of the back porch. However, the thought of that threatening animal made the Jack Russell terrier nervous. Wishbone knew he could take care of himself, but he still worried about what fate might befall Joe.

Joe reached down and scratched Wishbone's head, momentarily startling him. With a reassuring smile, Joe said, "I think that big dog's locked up, but maybe you'd better stay here, Wishbone. The bulldog might not like someone else coming into his yard."

Wishbone dutifully wagged his tail. "Thanks, Joe, but I know my doggie duty. It's you and I, buddy, side by side, to the bitter end."

Joe cautiously tried the gate. It was unlocked, kept shut by a strong spring that pinged and screeched in a rusty protest when he pushed. He stepped through, and Wishbone slipped inside, too. Joe didn't seem to notice him. All his attention was focused on the flagstone path, and at the end of it, on the six steps up to the porch and the big, dark brown mahogany front door.

Next door a lawnmower coughed and chugged to life with a *blat!* and a roar that made Wishbone jump. He got hold of himself and mentally told himself, *Easy, now, easy! Calm down. That noise is just Sean, starting his lawnmower.*

At the same moment, the bulldog came tearing around the house, bounding along in giant leaps. He gave one deep-throated bark. Wishbone had no time to think. Acting instinctively, he threw himself forward, crouching, ready to protect Joe. . . .

Joe shouted, "Wishbone, no!"

The bulldog charged! He dashed straight for Wishbone. . . .

Wishbone braced himself and let out a loud warning bark.

The bulldog skidded to a stop, looming over the smaller dog. . . .

And he licked his face!

Wishbone shook his head. "Hey! We haven't even been introduced!"

"Dewey!" It was a woman's voice. The bulldog turned and ran up the front steps, making happy grunting sounds. The front door opened, and framed in it stood the owner of the glowering face that had watched Joe and Sean practicing their basketball shots.

Taking a deep breath, Joe walked to the steps. They creaked under his sneakers, the old damp wood groaning beneath his weight.

"Well?" the woman asked. The bulldog had gone inside and sat behind her, looking up adoringly.

Wishbone smelled Joe's nervousness. He understood how frightened his friend had been when the bulldog charged, and how he dreaded speaking to the woman.

But at least Joe and I are standing side by side, facing the unknown dangers together. Just like Beowulf in his battle with the dreaded dragon—the old king had a trusted band of soldiers upon whom he relied to stand with him and help him.

Wishbone began to fantasize again, picturing to himself the scene as the aged Beowulf called together his most trusted warriors. The old king was preparing for the most dangerous and deadly battle of his life.

Chapter Ten

Fourteen men stood ready, all of them wearing chain-mail armor and helmets, all armed with swords, spears, or bows and arrows. Beowulf inspected them, feeling his heart lift with pride. *Fourteen went with me to kill Grendel all those years ago*, he thought. *Now fourteen fine warriors are ready to stand by my side against this new monster.* Among them was a sturdy young man named Wiglaf, who was barely twenty. He was Beowulf's cousin, though his father was a Swede, not a Geat. Wiglaf stood tall and rigid, but his eyes kept flickering admiringly toward the old king. *He has the energy of a young puppy*, Beowulf thought. *Just as I did once. May he thrive and grow strong and become a hero and a leader of men!*

Dressed in his heavy mail shirt, with his curved shield slung over his back on its strap, Beowulf paced back and forth before the selected squadron of soldiers, his nails clicking on the oak floor of his great hall. He glanced approvingly at their brawny arms.

They were battle-tested men, all of them wearing golden arm bands that spoke of their courage. Only Wiglaf had none, for Beowulf's reign had been a peaceful one for the last ten years or so. A few of the other men had fought under King Heardred, and one old soldier had even been a member of King Hygelac's army. *They are middle-aged,* Beowulf could not help thinking. *Still, they are men of courage and strength. I will have to trust them with my life.*

He sat before the men, his head lifted high, and raised a paw for attention. "My friends," he said, "I have lived a long time, and all my days I have been a warrior. I was only seven years old when King Hrethel, the father of Hygelac, took me into his army as a standard bearer. I carried his flag into many fights, and he rewarded me with gold. King Hrethel became a second father to me, treating me as an equal with his sons Herebeald, Haethcyn, and Hygelac. In later days I served Hygelac when he was king. You all know my story."

Wiglaf was smiling. He was proud of his older cousin, and he wanted to be just like him. Beowulf knew the feeling. In his youth, he had admired Hygelac. Desire for his king's approval had driven the young Beowulf to perform great deeds of daring.

The old king shook his head to clear the memories and said, "You've all heard of how I killed Grendel and Grendel's mother. I don't need to remind you of how I fought in the wars against the Swedes, because many of you stood beside me in those battles. I think I have proven myself."

"You have, my lord," replied a tall thane with a scar across his weathered face. "None here doubts your courage."

Beowulf nodded his thanks, his tail wagging slowly. "In the old times, we boasted before battle. Now I will do that again. You have heard how this night-flying dragon has murdered our people and set fire to our houses. He first struck Barrow-Town three nights ago. Two nights ago, we hear now, he burned four of our ships that were returning to harbor. Last night he attacked a village of farmers and shepherds, utterly destroying it. He will do so no more."

From its ornate sheath, Beowulf pulled a splendid sword, gleaming of blade and bright of grip. He reverently laid it before his men, letting them gasp at its beauty.

"This is Naegling," Beowulf announced. "Once I bore a wonderful weapon named Hrunting, and I thought that none would ever be better than that. But Naegling came to me in battle. I struck down a Swede who bore it, and I took it from him. In the days when giants walked the earth, the great blacksmith and weapon maker Wayland Smith himself forged Naegling. Men say that Wayland Smith was half a god—or that a god inspired him. Certainly he made a sword fit for Odin or Thor himself. Its match has never been forged."

"It is a marvelous sword," Wiglaf said, his voice hushed. "The worm has no chance against it."

Replacing the iron weapon in its scabbard, Beowulf

said, "If I could fight this dragon as I fought Grendel, I would. I would grapple with it, trusting my strong grip. But I expect hot fire and deadly venom in this melee, so I go in armor and helmet, and I will bear a sword and shield. Yet I will make this boast: Before allowing you to risk your own lives, I will meet the hill's guardian, this hateful dragon, in single combat. I will ask you to watch how I fare before you come to help me. If Fate gives me victory in the first exchange of blows, I will kill this creature and claim its treasure for our people. Still, we may be evenly matched. When once the beast and I have clashed, if you see I need aid, then draw your weapons and attack. Rally to me at that time of need and help me strike down the dragon. Either way, I promise you, come life or come death, I will not be the one to turn tail and run from this great fight."

"We will be ready to help you," Wiglaf promised.

Beowulf's tail wagged. "My thanks, young kinsman. My plan is to strike quickly. This dragon has come out only at night. I think if we draw it into the sunlight, it may be like an owl—its eyes may not see as well, and it may be confused. Let us set out!"

The men cheered. Beowulf took a deep breath, and he closed his eyes, as his sensitive nose detected the scents of iron and leather, the smells of men ready for battle. It had been a long time. *May Fate favor us all,* he thought.

Beowulf's warriors mounted horses and rode behind him as he trotted toward the site where Barrow-Town had once stood. As they traveled,

107

Beowulf looked around at the peaceful countryside. Farmers' cottages stood on both sides of the road, neat plowed fields behind them. The breath of spring was sweet in the air, and the budding trees were musical with the songs of birds. Geat-Land had once been a gloomy and forbidding place, a countryside of military camps and stone fortresses. Now it wore a softer, gentler face. Peace had brought blessings and rewards.

It was a sweet land, Beowulf thought, a country where men could be like brothers and live and work together. His reign had tamed the countryside. Men no longer needed to live like starving rats, fighting one another just to survive. Hrothgar had been right. A good king needed more than courage. He needed to be honest, fair, and just. Wealtheow, Hrothgar's queen, had also spoken truly when she had said that the greatest warrior was the one who brought peace to the land. Given that kind of leader, the land had prospered and grown beautiful.

Yet—Beowulf remembered with a faint smile—sometimes one had to be a wolf. Courage had to be there, strong stone under the gentle landscape. Without it, nothing could last, nothing could endure. Above all, a king must follow the commands of Fate. Looking back over the years, Beowulf felt humble. He had been hailed as the conqueror of Grendel and Grendel's mother—but Fate had been his friend then. Fate had determined their fall, not Beowulf. Would Fate serve him this day? He could only hope it would.

The unpaved road snaked through hilly country,

where vineyards of grapevines were turning green in the spring sun. Still higher, and the hills became stony, dark flint and weathered gray granite. From a height the war party could just glimpse the broad, dark sea, its surface streaked with white waves. *It is a beautiful world*, Beowulf thought. *I am happy that I have been allowed to live here and to enjoy it for so long. If Fate takes me today, at least it has spared me to see this beauty and to love it for a while.* Then he stopped, his nose coming up at the sharp, stinging stench of smoke.

The horses halted, too, as Wiglaf cried out and pointed. The dragon had visited this hillside. A shepherd's house—or the ruins of it—stood off to the left. The men rode slowly toward it, some of them nervously gripping the hilts of their swords. Beowulf took seven cautious steps, and his nose twitched. That sickening dragon-reek lay heavily over everything, a stench of flame and poison that nauseated him.

The hut had been stone-walled and thatch-roofed. The straw of the roof remained only as clumps of matted black ashes. Something powerful had ripped into the stone walls, pulling them down, breaking them wide as easily as a man could smash an eggshell. The doorway gaped open, its wooden door burned away, the iron hinges melted. Trails of molten iron had poured down the stone like splashes of candle wax and had hardened again, dull silvery-gray. Inside the door were heaps of burned furniture. Beowulf brought his nose to the stone wall. "It's still hot," he said. "This is one of the houses the dreaded dragon visited just last night."

One of the soldiers called the others over. He pointed to a muddy patch of ground near a ruin that had been the shepherd's well. A giant footprint impressed itself deeply in the mud there. It looked like the print of a great eagle's talon—an eagle impossibly vast. A claw of that size could seize a man the way a man could grip an apple. "How big is this monster?" the soldier asked, his voice trembling a little.

"It's as large as dragons grow," Beowulf said shortly, sniffing at the print. "This must be an old serpent, wily and strong. My counselor tells me that once dragons are fully grown, they can sleep for five hundred years between meals. When they wake up, though, they're ravenous. If we don't stop this creature, it might devour all of our countrymen."

"What about us?" another soldier asked.

"We're soldiers," Beowulf replied abruptly. "Risking death is our job." He barked an order, and everyone remounted. As the men rode on, they stayed closer together, and they kept glancing fearfully at the sky, as if they expected the dragon to come diving toward them at any moment.

The road descended, winding through a landscape of ruin and horror. More houses lay in shambles, some of them hardly more than jumbles of stones. No wooden buildings survived at all, not even the mead-hall of Barrow-Town. When the men arrived there, Beowulf groaned to see the wreckage. Only cellars and foundations remained of the houses. The dragon had seemingly spent most of his anger on the mead-hall. Had the beast sensed soldiers there, enemies that would try to kill it? Or was it only an unthinking creature taking out its anger on the largest building in the village? The mead-hall was a pile of smoldering ashes, red embers still glowing in its depths. Ten years earlier, Beowulf himself had paid to have the splendid hall constructed, and he had slept there that first night with the town guards.

Now nothing remained of the hall, and half the guards had died in the flaming ruin, burned alive while sleeping. A very few wretched refugees survived the fall of the town, but most of the population had died in the dragon's talons, or under the white-hot jets of its flaming breath.

With his heart feeling heavy, Beowulf thought,

Now I know just how Hrothgar felt so long ago when Grendel killed his men in Heorot. How bitter it is when a king cannot protect his people!

The soldiers searched through the ruins, gasping at the choking, bitter reek of dragon's breath. Unfortunately, they found no one alive. The people of Barrow-Town who remained had been reduced to nothing more than charred bone and ash.

"The cavern opening should be beyond those hills, overlooking the sea," Beowulf said, nodding to the east. "I asked Feodred for directions, and he gave them to me most carefully. Let's go have a look."

Barrow-Town had been built on a high plateau. On the east side, a rocky cliff dropped steeply away to the ocean a hundred feet below. As they approached the edge, Beowulf could hear the regular roaring of the surf. The restless ocean pounded against a narrow beach of black pebbles. A narrow path hewn into the stone led down the cliff face to the beach. It was barely wide enough for the warriors to travel in single file, but they did not have to go very far.

Feodred had told Beowulf that he had found a crevice in the stone there. It had been a slender opening barely wide enough to let him slip inside. Now the crevice was gone.

Something huge and powerful had burst from the cliff face. It had broken a great, jagged opening into the stone. Below, on the beach, blocks of granite, each the size of a small house, had fallen. Now a gaping cave mouth, thirty feet in diameter, pierced the cliff

wall, its top pointed and blackened. Thin wisps of oily black smoke drifted out. Beowulf's nose wrinkled. The creature lay inside, all right. His stomach lurched at the sickening stink of it.

He looked around. "I will try to lure the beast to the top of the cliff here," he said. "The ground is level and stony. I won't lose my footing, and the dragon will find no trees around me to burn." He pointed to a half-ruined stone wall, chest-high to a man, that once had offered protection to the people of Barrow-Town against any sea raiders climbing up from the beach. "Men, let Wiglaf lead your horses back to shelter in the ruins of the town. The rest of you must take cover behind the wall. I will go and offer a challenge to this serpent. May Fate be kind to us this day, and may the Geats gain glory from the battle to come."

The king waited until the men had done as he asked. When he saw Wiglaf returning on foot, he started down the treacherous path carved into the cliff. Beneath his paws the stone felt hot. Here and there great heat had cracked the granite, just the way a strong fire could crack glass. He came to the entrance of the cave and realized he could not go inside. The poisonous rankness of dragon breath was too strong. The very air inside the cavern was too hot. Beowulf could see the cliff face dancing in the waves of heated air pouring out of the cave.

Very well. If he could not venture inside, he would have to make the dragon come out to confront him. Hesitating only a moment, Beowulf threw back his head and howled a long, sharp battle cry. "Creature of darkness!" he barked. "Come to your doom! A hero waits for you—and Fate will see one of us die today! Come and try your strength and your skill against my keen blade and strong grip! Come to your doom!"

The echoes died away.

Then, from deep within the bowels of the earth a clamor and a snarling arose. Beowulf backed up the path to the top of the cliff. A roil of black smoke shot through with orange flame rolled out of the cave opening, and a shrieking bellow burst out, like the sound of doomsday itself.

The dragon had heard him.

And it was coming.

Chapter Eleven

The woman in the doorway said abruptly, "I don't have time to stand here all day!" She glanced at Joe. "Tell me your business or go away!"

Taking a deep breath, Joe said, "Uh . . . Mrs. Grindle, you don't know me, but I hung my backpack on your fence yesterday, and—"

"Oh, that was yours, was it?" She sniffed. "Just a minute." The door closed.

Joe looked down at Wishbone and shrugged. "I'll bet she's going to yell at me."

Wishbone gazed up. "Don't worry, Joe. Barking dogs don't bite! It's the tongue, see, it gets in the way—" Before Wishbone finished, Joe turned his gaze back to the door. Wishbone sighed. Why didn't people ever listen to the dog?

The boy and his dog stood on the porch for a minute. Two minutes. From next door came the drone of Sean's lawnmower. He was working on the far side of his house, though, so Joe and

Wishbone couldn't see him even from up on the hill.

Joe said, "I wonder if she's coming back."

Wishbone's ears flicked up and he turned his head. "Footsteps! She's coming back right now."

The door opened again, and Mrs. Grindle stood before them. She was a tall old woman, a head taller than Joe, with a ramrod-straight back. She had a cap of curly white hair, and she was wearing a dark maroon dress trimmed with black lace. Her expression was still a scowl. Her bright eyes glittered at the world from behind rimless spectacles, and her dark eyebrows were drawn down above them. Deep lines ran from her nose down to the corners of her mouth. "Dewey dragged it in," she said, holding out the backpack. "I wondered where he'd found it."

"It's mine," Joe said, sounding relieved. "Uh . . . I guess Dewey is the bulldog?"

"Dewey's my puppy," the woman explained, handing the backpack to Joe. "He went out yesterday afternoon, and later in the day I found this on the back steps. I didn't know where he'd found such a thing."

Wishbone could hardly believe his brown-spotted ears. A *puppy?*

"I'm sorry," Joe told Mrs. Grindle. "Sean and I were playing basketball next door yesterday afternoon, and I hung it on your fence. I guess your dog must have dragged it over somehow."

"He does love to play," Mrs. Grindle said, her

face softening. "So you were practicing your layups yesterday? How are you at rebounding?"

"Oh . . . I . . . I do all right . . . I guess," Joe stammered, sounding surprised.

"Humpf. You would do better if you'd focus on the ball, young man. Learn to keep one eye on the ball and the other on the court, and you'll do a *lot* better."

"I . . . uh . . . thanks. . . ." Joe started to turn, then stopped. "Excuse me, Mrs. Grindle, but how did you—I mean, you seem to know about basketball. . . ."

Mrs. Grindle rolled her eyes. "Well, I should hope so! There's a story there. Would you care to come inside?"

Joe glanced down. "Thanks, but I have my dog here."

"I noticed him. A Jack Russell, isn't he? That's a fine breed of dog."

Wishbone grinned. "For a monster, you're a very perceptive woman. Thank you!"

"Bring him in," Mrs. Grindle said. "I can't abide folks who never let their puppies inside. They act as if dogs were ill-mannered brutes, but they aren't if their owners don't make them that way. Come on. I'll show you something that might surprise you."

Joe looked uncertain, but when the woman stepped back, holding the door open, he went inside. Wishbone stayed right at his heel. His nose twitched as he discovered new aromas—furniture polish, a wool coat hanging in the hall closet, and the very strong scent of bulldog!

The bulldog himself came romping into the room. He stopped as soon as he saw Wishbone, then took two steps forward. Dewey didn't have much of a tail, but he wagged everything past his neck. Then he crouched down, his front legs flat on the floor, his wriggling rump high in the air. In doggie talk, he was saying, "Let's play!"

Wishbone took a few careful steps forward and the two curious canines sniffed noses. Dewey gave him a big slurp across the muzzle. Wishbone blinked. "Let's watch it, pal. You may be a great dog and everything, but that's twice you've moistened my muzzle!" Then Wishbone's nose twitched again. "Wait a minute. You've been eating Doggie Ginger Snaps! Any left?"

As if Dewey had understood Wishbone, the bulldog turned and ticktacked away through the house. Wishbone followed him down a short hall and into a tile-floored kitchen, where a big silvery bowl held a few Doggie Ginger Snaps. Dewey crunched one and watched as Wishbone approached.

"Well, I don't mind if I do, thanks." Wishbone took a treat and munched it happily. "Mmm! First-rate! Dewey, you're a dog after my own heart!"

The bowl wasn't very full, unfortunately, and the two dogs polished off the treats after only a few moments. Then Wishbone felt a little uneasy. He had promised to stand by Joe, but where was Joe? The faithful dog followed his nose to a study, two of its

walls lined with books. A tall trophy case held row
upon row of basketball trophies, and one wall sported
at least thirty black-and-white framed photographs of
girls' basketball teams.

"Fantastic!" Joe was saying. "You coached seven-
teen state championship teams?"

"Darned right I did," Mrs. Grindle said with
obvious pride. "I could have coached another half
dozen or so, but then the school board in my home-
town decided I had reached the mandatory retire-
ment age. They put me on the shelf ten years ago."
Mrs. Grindle sniffed. "I guess that soured me. The
next year my husband died, and then I inherited this
place from my older brother, so I came to Oakdale to
live. I've been pretty cranky, I suppose. Can't blame
people for avoiding me at first, and then by the time
I started to feel lonely, no one liked me. I've never
been good at making friends—except for Dewey,
right, my friend?"

Dewey, who had followed Wishbone in, barked approvingly.

Mrs. Grindle chuckled. "I think I would have curled up and died of loneliness without him. So your name's Talbot, is it? You wouldn't be related to the Talbot who was a coach, would you?"

"Yes. He was my dad," Joe said softly.

"He was a good coach," Mrs. Grindle said. "In fact, the advice I gave you was one of his sayings— 'Keep one eye on the ball, one eye on the court.' I know you must miss him. Did he ever tell you about the time his team was down to its last uninjured reserve player, behind twenty points at half-time? He gave the players a whale of a pep talk, and they won by two points in overtime."

"No," Joe said. "Did you know him?"

"Very well. I also admired him. He was a very bright and talented young man. By the way, how is your mother?"

Joe blinked in surprise. "You . . . you know my mother, too?"

"Slightly," Mrs. Grindle said. She wrinkled her forehead. "Hmm. Let me see. My heavens, the very last time I saw Ellen was at the Tri-State Athletic Banquet— oh, just before you were born. It's been a long time. I remember how proud she was of her husband and how much she was looking forward to having a baby." With a sigh, Mrs. Grindle added, "I wish I'd looked her up when I first moved to town, but that was in my bitter phase, when I just wanted to be left alone. It was foolish of me, because I really liked both your parents." She smiled. "In fact, I could tell you lots of stories about Coach Talbot: the time his team carried him through town on their shoulders; the boys he helped when no other coach would give them a chance."

"I'd really like to hear about all that," Joe admitted. For a moment he was quiet, and then he said, "Mrs. Grindle, do you need any help around the place?"

She tilted her head. "Hmm. I do have a touch of arthritis now. I can't keep the yard as tidy as I'd like. It's all I can do to keep the house and car neat! But I'm living on a pension, Joe. I couldn't afford to pay you."

"I wasn't thinking of that, exactly," Joe said. "But my friends like to play basketball, too. I thought maybe if we could come over and mow the lawn, get the roses in shape and stuff, you might give us some advice on playing."

Mrs. Grindle blinked. "Be an unofficial coach, you mean?"

Joe nodded. "We can use all the coaching we can get." He smiled. "You could tell me more about my dad, too."

For the first time, Mrs. Grindle smiled. Wishbone could not help smiling, too, in his own doggie way. So, the old gal wasn't a monster at all. When the scowl disappeared, Mrs. Grindle looked downright friendly, and even kind of shy. "I'd like that," she said softly. "I would like that more than I can tell you."

Wishbone jumped for joy, coming down gently on his front paws. "Did you hear that, Dewey? And here we were so scared—uh . . . I mean apprehensive—about meeting you. I've got a feeling you and I are going to be close friends! We'll share adventures together! We'll share excitement! We'll share some more of those delicious Doggie Ginger Snaps, if you have any left!"

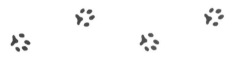

Everyone needs friends. Beowulf knew that already, but it had never been so obvious to him before he faced the dragon. Now there was a *real* monster. Unfortunately, the situation was so terrifying that it would test the friendship and loyalty of Beowulf's men . . . with some surprising results.

Chapter Twelve

Beowulf retreated up the path, keeping his sharp eyes on the dark cave opening. Another eruption of belching black smoke and flashing flame burst out, boiling upward into the sky. Behind it came a long, scaly, fanged snout. "Come on!" Beowulf shouted. "Here is a hero for you to eat— if you can! Come on!"

The old king backed up onto the cliff top, staring down with unbelieving eyes. Nothing could be that huge and move so fast! Like a gloppy green flood pouring from the opening, the dragon's long, snakelike body spilled out of the cave. Its batlike wings were folded along the ridge of its long spine. Its four talon-tipped legs seemed as if they were designed more to steady and balance the body than to propel it. The dragon crawled like a serpent, gripping the stone with its talons now and again. Its questing head came above the edge of the cliff, and then its body flowed up, coiling and writhing. Its huge eyes had

X-shaped pupils that had narrowed to thin black lines. It hissed, trying to turn its face away from the sunlight.

Beowulf drew his sword and stood his ground, gripping the hilt tightly in his teeth. He shrugged the shield around until it hung over his right shoulder, a position that would protect him as long as he could sense the jets of flame and maneuver quickly out of harm's way. The king clashed his sword against the shield once, twice, three times. The dragon's snakelike head whipped around, the black nostrils quivering, seeking out the hero's scent. The beast of darkness seemed almost blind in the sunlight.

It was far from helpless, though. Like lightning, the head drew back and then struck forward. The gaping mouth revealed row upon row of deadly fangs. Beowulf dropped to his belly, and a wash of flame broke over his shield, scorching his skin. He held his breath until the foul-smelling fire had passed and he saw the dragon's head darting in to bite. With all his might, the aging warrior swung Naegling, the swift sword that had never failed him.

Its bright blade clashed against the dragon's bony snout, bringing a bellow of rage and pain from the beast. It jerked its head away, scattering a spray of red blood as biting as acid. Drops of it hit the rock and bubbled, hissing as they ate pits into the stone. Beowulf backed away again, dismayed. Naegling's blade was discolored and dull where it had hacked the dragon's flesh. The king had hoped to end the battle with that blow, but the blade had not bitten deeply enough into its target.

The wounded dragon bellowed, coiled, and breathed a thin stream of fire. It could not see Beowulf, but it sensed him nearby, and it swept the cliff top with flame. Again the hero had to drop down and hide beneath his shield. He felt the pain of the fearsome fire and smelled the odor of his own singed fur. Gasping for breath, wincing against the poisonous vapors of the dragon's furious fire, he could not call for help.

Above Beowulf the dragon reared, spreading its wings, hissing deep inside its chest. From that great height the head plunged downward like a striking eagle. Beowulf had no chance to swing his sword. The blinding fire struck his shield and burned through it in three places. He cried out in pain as the deadly fire reached his hide, but he pressed forward, rolling over and over, barely evading the dragon's claws.

The hero looked back to his men at the wall. There Wiglaf, Beowulf's hero-worshipping young cousin, leaped to his feet. "It's time for us to help!" he shouted, drawing his sword. "Follow me!"

Beowulf saw him leap from the wall and run a few steps. Then, alone, Wiglaf spun and stared at the other thirteen men cowering behind the safety of the low stone wall.

"What's wrong with you? The king needs us!"

Wiglaf screamed, his voice sounding hoarse with frustration and fury. "You're his best men! He led you into battle, gave you rewards!" When the men only stared at him with wide, terrified eyes, Wiglaf sobbed. "Stay, you cowards! I go to die with my king!" Without another word, he raised his shield, gave a war cry, and ran toward the dragon.

"No!" Beowulf shouted. "It's too dangerous!"

The dragon hissed at the sound, but it still could not locate Beowulf. It reared back again, glaring at the ground, its head whipping from side to side on its long, snakelike neck. The king had plunged past it and lay in a hollow between two stones. He still gripped Naegling, but his shield—burned to a useless crisp—lay yards away, still smoldering.

Wiglaf ran straight to the king, shouting, "I'm here to help!" He thrust himself down on the ground, flat, beside Beowulf. "Don't worry," he said, panting. "Be the same hero you have always been, my king. Kill this dragon! I ask only that you let me help you, let me hold my shield to protect you from the beast's fire."

Trembling with pain, the old king could not speak. He nodded grimly and tightened his grip on Naegling. The dragon had finally seen them, and its head shot down like lightning.

Before the monster could breathe its flames, Beowulf leaped up, swinging Naegling as hard as he could. The sword caught the dragon at the corner of the jaw—and shattered. Beowulf's strong grip had not deserted him, but it proved to be an enemy now. Even the legendary Naegling could not survive the shock of that blow.

The wounded dragon bit the king along his back, causing him to cry out. But the dragon's jaw had been broken, too, and it could not close its mouth enough to kill Beowulf. It dropped him, bleeding, to the ground, then started to rear back in preparation for blowing another burst of flame.

Screaming with defiance, Wiglaf leaped forward, driving his sword point-first deep into the monster's neck. A welter of blood and flame burst out, and the wounded Beowulf quickly drew his battle knife from his belt. He plunged it again and again into the weeping wound, until the reeling dragon shook him free. It flapped its wings and tried to fly. No use. The creature was dying.

With a final bellow, it crashed full-length on the cliff top, and Wiglaf and Beowulf quickly cut the neck through behind the head, where it was thinnest. The enormous body jerked and twitched, and the jaw snapped twice. Then the headless body collapsed like a sail whose lines had been cut, and the light of life left those glaring golden eyes. The monster was dead.

Wiglaf stood and looked back toward the wall. No one was there. The terrified men had fled.

"Help me to that stone," Beowulf said, gasping for air.

"I will, my king. You have won!" Wiglaf stated

triumphantly. "Once again you have saved the Geats from a deadly enemy."

"Yes," Beowulf said, his chest heaving to draw breath into his burning lungs.

Wiglaf helped the senior warrior to a stone shaped almost like a throne, overlooking the water. Then the young man ran back to the other side of the wall, where a ruined well stood. He drew a pail of cold water and hurried back to his fallen king. With tender hands, he cleansed Beowulf's wounds. The old king did not flinch at Wiglaf's touch, but lay on the stone with his eyes looking out to sea.

"If I had a son," Beowulf said, "I would leave the kingdom to him."

"You will recover," Wiglaf replied, weeping. The people need you."

Beowulf shook his head. "No, my brave young friend. My wounds are too deep, and the monster's poison too powerful. I hear my ancestors calling me now, from somewhere out on that dark sea of eternity. Before night falls, I will join them."

"Please!" Wiglaf pleaded, sobbing.

"Don't grieve. I have had a long life and have served the Geats well. For many winters I have been their king, through ill and through good. At last I even brought them peace. Someone very wise once told me that the greatest warrior is he who brings peace to his people. A good king must be just, honest, and fair. Remember that when I am gone. Wiglaf, do you think you could explore that cavern? Before I leave the gold

of this world behind, I want to see some of the treasure
that will go to my people."

"Yes, my lord."

Wiglaf hurried away. Watching him, Beowulf
breathed deeply. He was not afraid any longer. The
choking stench of the dragon bothered him no more.
It seemed to him that both his eyes and nose were los-
ing their power. The day was growing dark, all smells
faint. The old king could no longer even feel the pierc-
ing pain of his wounds.

He knew the time was fast approaching when his
spirit would go forth on that last adventure. But some

power remained in him. He knew he could fight Death itself for a few minutes, could hold off that last enemy until young Wiglaf returned, bearing bright gold. "He stayed," the king murmured. "My tested warriors all ran away, and yet he stayed to fight by my side." He closed his weary eyes.

Perhaps he lost consciousness. When he opened his eyes again, he saw Wiglaf before him, holding a double armful of wonderful golden crowns, chains, and jeweled collars. "There is more," Wiglaf said, "so much more that it will take days to bring out."

Beowulf felt his heavy heart swell. he had

brought victory to his people one last time. A warrior could not ask much of Fate. He could only accept it. But then Beowulf breathed a silent prayer that Fate would favor young Wiglaf. A king might die, but courage could live on and on, generation to generation. Maybe someday, the old king thought, courage could grow great enough so that all the world might live in peace.

That would be the fairest Fate of all.

Beowulf was brave to the bitter end. He became a legendary hero, and his people always remembered him. Joe's courage paid off, too, leading to a busy, happy day. . . .

Chapter Thirteen

It was another beautiful Saturday morning, just one week after Joe had reclaimed his backpack. Wishbone came dashing around the Grindle house, and Dewey scampered along behind him. Wishbone glanced over his shoulder. "Uh-huh, pretty fast for a big guy. Let's see if you can do this!"

With a scrabble of claws, he reversed direction. The surprised bulldog braced his front paws, but his hind legs were a little slow to get the message. He flipped over! It was a soft fall, and he was up again in an instant, happily chasing Wishbone back around the house.

"They're playing tag!" Sam shouted, pruning the last rosebush into shape.

"Who's winning?" Sean asked with a big grin as he raked up grass clippings.

Joe shut off the lawnmower and then surveyed the level lawn with a touch of pride. "Maybe they both are."

Wishbone darted around the other side of the house, looked back expectantly, then dropped to the ground, panting. "I knew I could wear him out! Those big models are built for short runs. We sport models are made for endurance!" He looked around at the yard. "Nice job, guys! You'd hardly know this was the same place we visited a week ago! I'm glad my supervision paid off so well!"

"How's it coming, David?" Joe asked.

"Not bad, if I do say so myself. Just think, all of this was done with scrap wood and a couple of quarts of leftover white paint!" David had built some graceful white wooden trellises, and he and Sam were putting the last one up, tying the trimmed rosebush to the laths so the flowers would climb and blossom.

"Too bad we can't paint the house, too," Joe said. "That would make the whole place just about perfect."

"Oh, didn't I tell you?" Sam called over. "I talked to Ms. Gilmore about that. You know, Mrs. Grindle was a Windom before she married, and the Windoms were important people in Oakdale. Ms. Gilmore agrees that this is a historic house, and she's rounding up some members of the Historical Society to paint and do some repairs. She's already persuaded the hardware store to donate the paint."

Wishbone grinned. "Wanda can be very persuasive, all right. If I could just persuade her that her yard needs a hole in it now and then, we would get along just great!"

134

David stood back and surveyed the neat row of trellises. "These really do brighten up the place."

"They're wonderful, David," Mrs. Grindle agreed heartily. She had come out quietly onto the porch, and now she stood looking proudly at the yard. "A trim lawn and neat flowerbeds make a world of difference. I'm ashamed I let this place run down that way!"

Ellen Talbot came out behind her, holding a tray with a frosty pitcher and a stack of plastic tumblers. "You've all worked hard. Ready for a lemonade break?"

"Great!" Sam said enthusiastically.

Soon everyone was sitting on the porch steps, sipping cold, tangy home-made lemonade.

Mrs. Grindle was relaxing in a porch chair admiring the yard. "I can't get over how much you've done," she said with admiration.

"It wasn't so bad," Sean replied shyly, between sips of his lemonade. The afternoon before, dressed in sweats and with a whistle dangling around her neck on a chain, Mrs. Grindle had shown him about six ways to strengthen his already fabulous layup shot. The improvement had really impressed Wishbone, and he was looking forward to the next week, when they were going to start on rebounds!

"Thank you," Mrs. Grindle said softly. "I was such an old fool to let people make me think that because my school career was over, no one wanted to be around me anymore. I'm just beginning to realize how much I have missed having young friends these past few years."

Joe looked at his mother and grinned. "Have you asked her?"

Ellen laughed. "Thelma, Joe thought it would be nice if you could come over for a pot-roast dinner tonight, and I agreed that it was a great idea. We'd love to have you, and we can catch up on old times."

Again Mrs. Grindle gave them her shy smile. "I'd be delighted," she said softly, "but only if I can bring Dewey over, too. He gets very lonesome without me."

Wishbone leaped up. "Sure you can! We can share my dinner bowl, and we can play, and I'll take him over to Wanda's yard and show him all the best places for digging!" Wishbone looked up at Ellen, stepping eagerly from side to side. "Say Dewey can come, Ellen, oh, please-please-please-please, please!"

Ellen nodded, looking happy. "Of course Dewey can come! He'll be great company for Wishbone. Look at him dancing around. You'd almost think he understands everything we're saying."

"That's because I listen, Ellen!" Wishbone took off, racing down the porch steps and running around the house to the spot where Dewey had flopped to rest in the sun. Wishbone thought Dewey was probably ready to play again—after all, he had been resting for nearly five whole minutes!

He ran around the corner and rushed over to his new friend. A good meal, more games of chase, and Wanda's flowerbeds were all just waiting to be savored. The two pooch pals were going to have a *lot* of fun together!

About Anonymous

*B*eowulf was composed by an unknown poet, so you would think we wouldn't know very much about the author. In a way that's true, but we can make some educated guesses. To begin with, the poet was probably a scop, or court poet. The Old English poem *Widsith* gives us a good idea of what such a poet was like. He went from place to place, searching for a king who would give him a home. In return, the poet entertained the nobles with his songs and even wrote songs about the king, so that the king's fame "may last under heaven."

Picture an English banquet hall in the dead of winter. Outside, snow falls and the wind howls. Inside, the atmosphere is stuffy, crowded, and noisy as people eat and talk loudly to their neighbors. Then a short, slight man seated near the king rises, holding a small harp. Everyone falls silent. He begins to play a melody on the harp, and in a clear, high voice he sings the words of a heroic poem. Everyone listens attentively, imagining the action of the poem—battles and raids, monsters and great deeds. After a few minutes, the scop ends his song and sits again, and people nod their appreciation.

The scop was essentially an entertainer, of course, but he was much more than that. He was the memory of the people at a time when very few people knew how to read or write. His songs were an important part of the oral tradition of storytelling. They kept the past alive and made history seem real. If the scop was very good at his craft—like the one who first sang about Beowulf—his poem would last and become part of our literature. That is why, more than one thousand years after the tale was first told, we can read today of Beowulf's heroism, strength, and sacrifice.

About *Beowulf*

An early classic of English literature, *Beowulf* was probably first composed as an oral poem sometime between 550 A.D. and 750 A.D. It was written down by someone—most likely a monk—in the tenth century A.D. Scholars are able to estimate these dates because of specific historical references made in the poem, and also because of the fact that the writer added Christian commentary to the story. At the time of *Beowulf*, however, neither the Danes nor the Geats would have been Christianized. They would have worshipped the old Norse gods: among them Odin, Thor, and Freya.

Beowulf exists in only one manuscript, and that manuscript has had some close calls. In 1731, the British library in which it was stored caught fire. Although someone carried the ancient poem to safety, it was badly scorched. The manuscript has deteriorated since that time, with parts of it flaking away. Fortunately, a Danish scholar named Thorkelin had two copies of the poem made in 1786, before the damage became too severe. Since he lived long before the invention of photocopy machines or cameras, these two copies of the 3,200-line poem had to be written carefully in longhand.

Then, as if the poem had some lingering evil curse on it left over from the days of the monster Grendel and his mother, Thorkelin's exhaustive twenty-year study and analysis of *Beowulf* suffered a serious setback during the Napoleonic wars. A British bombardment of Copenhagen, Denmark, in 1807 destroyed all of Thorkelin's valuable notes on the poem! Luckily, his copies were not damaged, and he used them to issue the first published edition of *Beowulf* in 1815. Today, the original, fire-damaged manuscript is carefully protected in the British Museum in London, England, and many different translations of the Old English poem have appeared.

Because *Beowulf* gives us only a hazy glimpse into long-forgotten times, the epic poem continues to fascinate readers. Although we may no longer believe that mythical dragons and monsters dwell in the fog-shrouded swamps, we can experience the mystery and sadness of the poem. We can also appreciate the literary masterpiece's underlying universal messages: courage in the face of great odds, loyalty even in the teeth of terror, and friendship to the very end.

About Brad Strickland

Brad Strickland is a writer and college professor who lives in Oakwood, Georgia. As an associate professor of English at Georgia's Gainesville College, he has often taught *Beowulf* and is always stirred by the poem's heroics. He is sure that a daring character like Wishbone would find the tale a fascinating adventure.

In addition to writing *Be a Wolf!*, Brad has authored *Salty Dog*, a Wishbone adventure based on Scottish writer Robert Louis Stevenson's classic pirate tale, *Treasure Island.* He has also written or co-written twenty-two other novels, fifteen of them for young readers. Brad's first young-adult novel was *Dragon's Plunder*, a story of adventure on the high seas. With his wife, Barbara, Brad has co-written stories for the *Star Trek* and *Are You Afraid of the Dark?* novel series. He also co-wrote four books with the late John Bellairs, and he continues to write books in Bellairs's popular young-adult mystery series, most recently *The Hand of the Necromancer.*

Brad and Barbara have two children, Jonathan and Amy. In addition to teaching and writing, Brad enjoys photography, travel, and amateur acting. In fact, he once played the role of a dragon on radio—and remembering that role helped him get in the mood to write the exciting last part of the *Be a Wolf!* story. The Strickland family is home to a menagerie of pets, including cats, ferrets, a rabbit, and two dogs, neither of which has so far shown much interest in books.